# GRANNY
# DAN

## *Also by Danielle Steel*

# Danielle Steel

# Granny Dan

Delacorte  Press

LARGE PRINT EDITION

Published by
Delacorte Press
Random House, Inc.
1540 Broadway, New York, New York 10036

Library of Congress Cataloging in Publication Data
Steel, Danielle.
    Granny Dan / Danielle Steel.
        p.   cm.
    ISBN 0-385-31709-3   ISBN 0-385-33427-3 (lg. print)
    1. Soviet Union—History—Revolution, 1917–1921—Fiction.
2. Russian Americans—Fiction.   I. Title.
PS3569.T33828G73   1999
813'.54—dc21      98-31932
                                                            CIP

Manufactured in the United States of America
Published simultaneously in Canada
June 1999
10   9   8   7   6   5   4   3   2   1
BVG

This Large Print Book carries the
Seal of Approval of N.A.V.H.

To Great Loves,
and small ballerinas,
each cherished separately,
and carried in the heart
forever.

And to Vanessa,
most specially,
so much loved child,
and extraordinary
ballerina.
May life treat you with
grace, kindness, and
compassion.

With all my love,
d.s.

# GRANNY
# DAN

# *Prologue*

*T*he box arrived on a snowy afternoon two weeks before Christmas.
It was neatly wrapped, tied with string, and
was sitting on my doorstep when I came
home with the children. We had stopped in
the park on the way home, and I had sat on
a bench, watching them, thinking of her
again, as I had almost constantly for the last
week since her service. There was so much
about her I had never known, so much I
had only guessed at, so many mysteries to
which only she held the key. My greatest
regret was not asking her about her life
when I had the chance, but just assuming it
wasn't important. She was old, after all,
how important could it be? I thought I
knew everything about her.

She was the grandmother with the dancing eyes who loved to roller-skate with me, even into her late eighties, who baked exquisite little cookies, and spoke to the children in the town where she lived as though they were grown up and understood her. She was very wise, and very funny, and they loved her. And if they pressed her to, she did card tricks for them, which always fascinated them.

She had a lovely voice, played the balalaika, and sang beautiful old ballads in Russian. She always seemed to be singing, or humming, always moving. And to the very end, she was lithe and graceful, loved by all, and admired by everyone who knew her. The church had been surprisingly full for a woman of ninety. Yet none of us really knew her. None of us understood who she had been, or where, or the extraordinary world she had come from. We knew she had been born in Russia and that she arrived in Vermont in 1917, and that she had married my grandfather sometime later. We just assumed she had always been there, part of our lives, just as she was. As one does about old people, we assumed she had always been old.

None of us really knew anything about her, and what lingered in my head were the unanswered questions. All I could ask myself now was why I had never thought to ask her. Why had I never sought the answers to the questions?

My mother had died ten years before and perhaps even she hadn't known the answers or wanted to know them.

My mother had been far more like her father, a serious sort, a sensible woman, a true New Englander, although her father wasn't. But like him, she was a woman of few words and impenetrable emotions. Little said, little known, and seemingly uninterested in the mysteries of other worlds, or the lives of others. She went to the supermarket when there were specials on tomatoes and strawberries, she was a practical person who lived in a material world, and had little in common with her own mother. The word that best described my own mother was *solid,* which is not the word anyone would have used to describe her mother, Granny Dan, as I called her.

Granny Dan was magic. Granny Dan seemed to be made up of air and fairy dust and angel wings, all things magical and luminous and graceful. The two women seemed to have nothing in common with each other, and it was always my grandmother who drew me to her like a magnet, whose warmth and gentleness touched my heart with countless unspoken graceful gestures. It was Granny Dan I loved most of all, and whom I was missing so desperately that snowy afternoon in the park, wondering what I would do without her. She had died ten days before, at ninety.

When my mother died at fifty-four, I was sorry, and knew I would miss her. I would miss the stability she represented to me, the reliability, the place to come home to. My father married her best friend the year after she died, and even that didn't particularly shock me. He was sixty-five, had a bad heart, and needed someone there at night to cook him dinner. Connie was his oldest friend and a sensible stand-in for my mother. It didn't bother me. I understood. I never pined for my mother. But Granny Dan . . . the world had lost some of its magic for me, knowing she was no longer in it. I knew I would never hear her sing again, in the lilting Russian. . . . The balalaika was long gone by then. But with her went a special kind of excitement. I knew that my children would never understand what they had lost. She was just a very old woman to them, with kind eyes, and a funny accent . . . but I knew better. I knew exactly what I'd lost, and would never find again. She was an extraordinary human being, a mystical kind of soul. Once one had met her, one could not forget her.

The package sat on the kitchen table for a long time, while the children clamored for dinner and watched TV as I prepared it. I had been to the supermarket that afternoon, and bought what I needed to make Christmas cookies with them. We had planned to make them together that night, so they could take them to school to their teachers. Katie wanted to make cupcakes instead. But Jeff and Matthew had agreed to make Christmas bells with red and green sprinkles. It was a good night to do it, because Jack, my husband, was out of town. He was in Chicago for three days of meetings. He had come to the funeral with me the week before and had been warm and sympathetic. He knew how much she meant to me, but as people do, he had tried to point out that she'd had a good, long life, and it was reasonable that she move on now. Reasonable to him, but not to me. I felt cheated to have lost her, even at ninety.

Even at ninety, she was still pretty. She wore her long, straight white hair in a braid down her back, as she always had, and wrapped it tightly in a bun for important occasions. All her life she had worn her hair that way. In my eyes, all her life she had looked the same. The straight back, the slim figure, the blue eyes that danced when she looked at you. She had made the same cookies I had planned to make that night, had shown me how to do them. But when she made them, she wore her roller skates and zipped gracefully around her kitchen. She made me laugh, she made me cry sometimes with her wonderful stories about ballerinas and princes.

She had taken me to the ballet for the first time. And if I had had the chance as a child, I would have loved to dance with her. But there was no ballet school where we lived in Vermont, and my mother didn't want her to teach me. She had tried in her kitchen once or twice, but my mother thought it was more important to do home-work and chores, and help my father out with the two cows he kept in the barn. Un-like her mother, she didn't have much whimsy. Dancing was not part of my life as a child, nor music. The magic and the mys-tery, the grace and art, the curiosity about a broader world than mine, was brought to me by Granny Dan as I sat listening to her for hours in her kitchen.

She always wore black. She seemed to have an endless supply of frayed black dresses and funny hats. She was neat and precise, and had a kind of natural elegance. But she never had an exciting wardrobe.

Her husband, my grandfather, had died when I was a child, from an attack of influ-enza that turned into pneumonia. I asked her if she loved him, once when I was twelve, I mean . . . really loved him. . . . She had looked startled when I asked her that, and then slowly she smiled at me, and hesitated for a moment before she answered.

"Of course I did," she said with the gentle Russian accent. "He was very good to me. He was a fine man." It wasn't really what I wanted to know. I wanted to know if she had been madly in love with him, like one of the princes in the stories she told me.

My grandfather had never seemed particularly handsome to me, and he was much older than she was. In the pictures I'd seen, he looked a lot like my mother, serious and somewhat stern. People didn't smile in photographs in those days. They made it seem very painful. And it was hard for me to imagine him with her. He had been twenty-five years older than she was. She met him when she arrived in America from Russia in 1917. She worked in the bank he owned, and he had lost his wife years before. He had no children and hadn't remarried, and Granny Dan always said he'd been very lonely when she met him, and very kind to her, but she never explained it. She must have been beautiful then, and in spite of himself, he must have been dazzled by her. They were married sixteen months after they met. My mother was born a year after that, and they never had any other children. Just one, and he doted on my mother, probably because she was so much like him. I knew all that, always had. What I didn't know, not clearly anyway, was what had come before it. Who Granny Dan had been when she was young, precisely where she had come from or why. The historical details had seemed unimportant to me as a child.

I knew she had danced with the ballet in St. Petersburg, and met the Czar, but my mother didn't like her to tell me about it. She said it would fill my head with wild ideas about foreigners and places I would never see, and my grandmother respected her daughter's wishes. We talked about the people we knew in Vermont, the places I'd been, the things I did in school. And when we went ice-skating on the lake, she would look dreamy-eyed for a moment at first, and I always knew she was thinking of Russia and the people she knew there. It didn't matter what she said, or didn't say, they were still very much a part of her, a part I loved and longed to know, a part I sensed even then was still important to her, more than fifty years after she'd left them. I knew that her entire family, her father and four brothers, had died in the war and the Revolution, fighting for the Czar. She had come to America and never seen any of them again, and made a new life in Vermont. But still, for a lifetime, the people she had known and loved had remained woven into the fiber of her being, part of the tapestry of her life, a part that could not be denied, even though she hid it.

I found her toe shoes in the attic one day, looking for an old dress of hers to wear for a school play, and they were just sitting there, in an open trunk in the attic. They were well-worn, and seemed tiny in my hand. The threadbare toes seemed magical as I gently touched the satin, and later I asked her about them.

"Oh," she said, looking startled at first, and then she laughed, looking suddenly young as she thought about them. "I wore them on the last night I danced with the ballet in St. Petersburg at the Maryinsky. . . . The Czarina was there . . . and the Grand Duchesses." This time she forgot to look guilty as she said it. "We danced *Swan Lake*," she said, her mind a million miles away as she thought about it. "It was a beautiful performance. . . . I didn't know it would be my last then. . . . I don't know why I kept the slippers. . . . It's all so long ago now, my love." She seemed to shut the door on the memories, and then handed me a cup of hot chocolate with lots of whipped cream on it, and little shavings of chocolate and cinnamon.

I wanted to ask her more about the ballet, but she disappeared for a while, and came back with her embroidery while I was doing my homework in her kitchen. I didn't get the chance that night, and it didn't come up again, not for years anyway. And eventually, I forgot about them. I knew she had danced with the ballet, we all did, but it was hard for me to imagine her as a prima ballerina. She was my grandmother, Granny Dan, the only grandmother in town with her own roller skates. She wore them proudly with one of her plain little black dresses, and when she went downtown, particularly to the bank, she always wore a hat and gloves, her favorite earrings, and looked as though she were going to do something important. Even when she picked me up at school in her ancient car, she looked dignified, and so happy to see me. It was so easy to see who she was then, and so much harder to remember who she had been. But I realize now that she had never wanted us to remember. She was by then who she had become, my grandfather's widow, my mother's mother, my grandmother who made Russian cookies. Anything beyond that was too much to dream, too much to even fathom.

I wondered if Granny Dan lay awake at night, thinking of the past, and remembering what it felt like to dance *Swan Lake* for the Czarina and her daughters? Or had she let it all go years before, grateful for the life she had with all of us in Vermont? Her two lives had been extraordinarily different. So much so that it allowed us all to forget her past, to believe that she was someone different now, rather than who she had been in Russia. And she let us believe that, for all the years we knew her. In turn, we allowed her to forget about it, or forced her to, and we made her be the person it was comfortable for us to think she was. In my eyes, she had never been young. In my mother's, she had never been beautiful and glamorous and a ballerina. In her husband's, she had never been anything but his. He didn't even like hearing about her father and brothers. They were part of a world he no longer wanted her to be part of. Perhaps he didn't want her to remember.

She was his, until he died, and left her to us. But she was mine, more than my mother's. They were never close, but we were. The beloved grandmother who meant everything to me . . . whose whimsy made me what I am, whose visions gave me the courage to leave Vermont. I went to New York after college, found a job in advertising, got married eventually, and had three children. I am married to a good man, have a life I love, and haven't worked in seven years. I'm planning to go back to work one day, when the children are a little older, when they don't need me at home so much, when I no longer feel I should be at home with them, making cookies.

When I grow up, when I grow old, I want to be like Granny Dan one day. I want to wear roller skates in my kitchen, and go ice-skating, which I did with her and still love to do. I want to make my children and grandchildren smile, and remember the things I did for them. I want them to remember the Christmas bells, and decorating the tree with me, and the hot chocolate I make just like hers, while they do their homework. I want my life to mean something to them, and I want the time I spend with them to make a difference. But I want them to know who I was, too, and why I came here, and that I love their father very much.

There are no mysteries in my life, no hidden stories, no victories like hers, dancing *Swan Lake* in the final hours of Imperial Russia. I cannot even imagine now what her life must have been, or how much she must have given up when she came here. I cannot imagine never speaking of it again, and losing all the people you love. I cannot imagine moving to a place like Vermont when you come from Russia. And I wish I knew why she never spoke of it to me, more than she did. Perhaps only because we did not want her to be Danina Petroskova, the ballerina. We only wanted her to be Granny Dan, we only wanted her to be our mother and wife and grandmother. It was easier for us that way, there was nothing for us to live up to. We didn't have to feel that we were less than her earlier life had been, or than she was. We didn't have to know, or feel, her pain, or grief, or loss, or mourn who she had been, if we never knew her. But now, as I think of her, I wish I had known more about her. I wish I could have seen her then, wish I could have been there with her.

I put the package aside while I made the Christmas bells with Jeff and Matt, and got the green and red sprinkles all over me. And then afterward, I made cupcakes with Katie and she managed to get the icing all over herself, me, and the kitchen.

It was late by the time I got everyone into bed, and Jack called me from Chicago. He had had a long day, but his meetings had gone well. I had forgotten the package completely by then, and only remembered it when I went to get something to drink in the kitchen after midnight. It was still sit-

ting there, off to the side, with a little cup-
cake batter on the string, and a thin veil of
green and red sprinkles.

I took the box in my hands, dusted it
off, and sat down at the kitchen table with
it. It took me a few minutes to undo the
string and open it. It was from the nursing
home where Granny Dan had spent her last
year. I had already picked up all her things,
when I stopped by, to thank them after the
service. Most of her things had been well-
worn, and there had been very little worth
keeping, just a lot of pictures of the kids,
and a small stack of books. I had kept one
book of Russian poetry I knew she loved,
and left the rest of them for the nurses. All
I saved of hers, of importance to her, was
her wedding ring, her gold watch that my
grandfather had given her before he married her, and a pair of earrings. She had
told me once that the watch had been the
first gift my grandfather had ever given her.
He'd never been particularly generous with
her, in terms of gifts or trinkets, although
he had provided well for her. There was an
old lace bed jacket that I had brought home
with me too, and slipped into the back of

my closet. But everything else was donated. So now I couldn't imagine what they had sent me.

As the paper peeled away, it revealed a large, square box, about the size of a hat box, and as I picked it up, it was heavy. The note said they had found it at the top of her closet, and they wanted to be sure I got it. And as I lifted off the lid, not sure what I'd find, I caught my breath sharply when I saw them. They were just as I remembered, the toes worn and a little frayed, the ribbons that had gone around her ankles pale and faded. They were her toe shoes. Just as I had seen them years before in her attic. The last pair she had worn before leaving Russia. There were other things in the box as well, a gold locket with a man's photograph in it. He had a well-trimmed beard and a mustache, and in a serious, old-fashioned way, he looked very handsome. He had eyes like hers, which all these years later seemed to laugh out of the photograph, in spite of the fact that he wasn't smiling. There were photographs of other men as well, in uniforms, and I guessed them to be her father and brothers. One of the boys looked incredibly like her. And there was a small, formal portrait of her mother, which I think I'd seen once before. There was the program from her last *Swan Lake*, a photograph of a cluster of smiling ballerinas, and a young beauty at the center of them whose eyes and face had never changed in all the years since then. It was easy to see that it was Danina. She looked breathtakingly beautiful and incredibly happy. She was laughing in the photograph, and all the other women were looking at her with affection and admiration.

And in the bottom of the box was a thick packet of letters. I could see at a glance that they were in Russian, in a neat, elegant hand that looked both masculine and intelligent. They were tied together with a faded blue ribbon and there were a great many of them. And I knew as I held them that the answer to the mystery was there, the secrets she had never told, or shared, once she left Russia. So many smiling faces there, in that box, so many people she had once cared about, and had left, for a life that couldn't possibly have been more different for her.

I held the toe shoes in my hand, and gently stroked the satin, thinking about her. How brave she had been, how strong, and how much she had left behind her. I couldn't help wondering if any of them were still alive, if she had meant as much to them, if they still had pictures of her. And I mused silently about the man who had written the letters to her, what he had been to her, and what had happened to him. But just from the careful way she had tied the bow, saved the letters for nearly a century, and took them to the nursing home with her, I knew without being able to read them. He must have been important to her, and from all he had written to her, I guessed easily that he must have loved her dearly.

She had had another life before she came to us, long before she came to me. A life so different from what we had seen of her, in Vermont, a life once filled with magic and excitement and glamor. I remembered how stern my grandfather had looked in his photographs, and hoped that this man had brought happiness to her, that he had loved her. She had taken his secrets to her grave with her, and now left them to me . . . with the toe shoes . . . the program from *Swan Lake* . . . and his letters.

I looked at his photograph again then, in the locket, and knew instinctively that the letters were from him. And once again, I burned with a thousand questions. There would be no one to answer them. I thought instantly about having the letters translated, so that I would know what they said. Yet at the same time I sensed that invading the secrets held in them would be a kind of intrusion on her. She hadn't given them to me. She had simply left them. But knowing how close we had been, I hoped she wouldn't mind it. We had been kindred spirits. She had left behind a thousand memories for me, of times we had shared, things we had done, legends and fairy tales she had told me. Perhaps along with the legends, she would not mind sharing this part of her story with me. At least, I hoped not. And my excitement over finding the letters and the photographs began to burn like a flame I could not dim. There was no running away from the truths she had hidden for a lifetime.

In my eyes, she had always been old, always been mine, always been Granny Dan. But in another time, another place, there had been dancing, people, laughter, love. She had left only a whisper of it with me, to remind me that she had once been young. And as I finally came to understand that, I sat looking at the smiling face of the young ballerina in the photograph, and a tear of longing for her rolled down my face, as I smiled, and held the faded pink toe shoes she had left me. And as the ancient pink satin touched my cheek, I looked at the neat stacks of letters tied with ribbons, hoping that at last I would know her story. I sensed with my entire being that there was much to tell.

# Chapter 1

$D$anina Petroskova was born in 1895 in Moscow. Her father was an officer in the Litovsky Regiment, and she had four brothers. They were tall and handsome and wore uniforms, and brought her sweets when they came home to visit. The youngest of them was twelve years older than she was. And when they were at home, they sang and played with her, and made lots of noise. She loved being with them, passed from one pair of powerful shoulders to the other, as they ran with her, and let her pretend that they were her horses. It was obvious to Danina, as it was to everyone, that her brothers adored her.

What Danina remembered of her mother was that she had a lovely face and gentle ways, she wore a perfume that smelled of lilac, and she would sing Danina to sleep at night, after telling her long, wonderful stories about when she was a little girl herself. She used to laugh a lot, and Danina loved her. She died when Danina was five, of typhoid. And after that, everything changed in Danina's life.

Her father had absolutely no idea what to do about her. He wasn't equipped to take care of a child, particularly one so young, and a girl child. He and his sons were in the army, so he hired a woman to take care of her, a string of them, but after two years, he knew he simply couldn't do it anymore. He had to find another solution for Danina. And he found the perfect one, he thought. He went to St. Petersburg to make the arrangements. He was vastly impressed when he spoke to Madame Markova. She was a remarkable woman, and the ballet school and company she ran would provide not only a home for Danina but a useful life, and a future she could rely on. If it became clear to them eventually that Danina had real talent, she would have a life with them, for as long as she could dance. It was a grueling life, and one that would require great sacrifices of her, but his wife had loved the ballet, and he sensed deep in his soul that the child's mother would have been pleased with his solution. It would be costly for him to keep her there, but he felt the sacrifice he'd have to make was worth it, particularly if in time she became a great dancer, which he considered likely. She was an unusually graceful little girl.

Danina's father and two of her brothers took her to St. Petersburg in April, after she turned seven. There was still snow on the ground, and as she stood looking up at her new home, her entire body trembled. She was terrified and she didn't want them to leave her there. But there was nothing she could do to stop them, nothing she could say or do. She had already begged her father, while they were still in Moscow, not to send her away to live with the ballet. He had told her it was a great gift to her, an opportunity that would change her life, and she would be a great ballerina one day, and be happy she had gone there.

But on that fateful day, she could imagine none of it. All she could think of was not the life she was gaining, but the cherished one she had lost. She stood holding her own small suitcase, as an elderly woman opened the door. She led them down a dark hallway, and Danina could hear shouting in the distance, music, and voices, and something hard and terrifying tapping loudly on a floor. The sounds all around her were ominous and strange, the halls they passed through dark and cold, until at last they reached the office where Madame Markova was waiting for them. She was a woman with dark hair, which she wore in a severe bun, a deathly pale, unlined face, and electric blue eyes that seemed to look right through her. Danina wanted to cry the moment she saw her, but she didn't dare. She was too frightened.

"Good morning, Danina," Madame Markova said sternly. "We have been expecting you," she said, sounding to the child like the devil at the gates of hell. "You will have to work very hard if you wish to live with us," Madame Markova warned her, as Danina nodded, with a huge lump in her throat. "Do you understand me?" She spoke very clearly, and Danina looked up at her with eyes filled with terror. "Let me look at you," she said then. She came around the desk in a long black skirt, which she wore over a leotard, with a short black jacket. Her entire outfit was the same color as her hair. She looked at Danina's legs then, and pulled up her skirt to see them better, and seemed satisfied with what she saw there. She glanced at Danina's father, and nodded. "We will let you know how she is doing, Colonel. The ballet is not for everyone, as I have told you."

"She's a good girl," he said kindly, and both her brothers smiled proudly.

"You may leave us now," Madame Markova said then, well aware that the child was about to panic. All three men kissed her, as tears streamed from Danina's eyes. And a moment later, they left her alone in the office with the woman who would now rule her life. There was a long silence in the room after they left, as neither teacher nor child spoke, and the only sound between them was Danina's stifled sobs.

"You do not believe me now, my child,

but you will be happy here. One day this will be the only life you will want or know." Danina looked at her with agonized suspicion, and then Madame Markova stood up, came around her desk, and held out a long, graceful hand. "Come, we will go to watch the others." She had taken in children this young before. In fact, she preferred it. If they had a gift, it was the only way to truly train them properly, to make it their only life, their only world, the only thing they wanted. And there was something about this child that intrigued her, there was something luminous and wise about her eyes. She had a kind of magic and whimsy about her, and as they walked down the long, cold halls hand in hand, far above Danina's head the older woman smiled with pleasure.

They stopped in each class for a little while, beginning with those who were already performing. Madame Markova wanted her to see what she had to strive for, the excitement of the way they danced, the perfection of their style and discipline. From there, they moved on to the younger dancers, who were already very creditable performers and might well inspire her. And at last, they stopped at the class of students with whom Danina would study, exercise, and dance. Danina couldn't begin to imagine being able to dance with them, as she watched, then jumped in terror as Madame Markova rapped hard on the floor with the cane she carried for just that purpose.

The teacher signaled her class to stop, and Madame Markova introduced Danina and explained that she had come from Moscow to live at the school with the others. Now she would be the youngest student, and the most childlike. The others had a strict, disciplined quality that made them seem older than they were. The youngest student was a nine-year-old boy from the Ukraine, and Danina was only seven. There were several girls who were nearly ten, and one who was eleven. They had already been dancing for two years, and Danina would have to work hard to catch up with them, but as they smiled at her and introduced themselves, Danina began to smile shyly. It was like having many sisters, instead of only brothers, she thought suddenly. And when they took her to see her place in the dormitory after lunch, she felt like one of them when they showed her her bed. It was small and hard and narrow.

She went to sleep that night thinking of her father and her brothers. She couldn't help but cry, missing them, but the girl in the next bed, hearing her cry, came to comfort her, and soon there were several others sitting on her bed with her. They sat with her and told her stories, of ballets, and wonderful times they had shared, of dancing *Coppelia* and *Swan Lake,* and seeing the Czar and Czarina come to a performance. They made it all sound so exciting that Danina listened to them intently and forgot her miseries, until at last she fell asleep while they were still talking to her about how happy she would be there.

And in the morning, they woke her at five o'clock with the others, and gave her her first leotard and ballet shoes. They ate breakfast every morning at five-thirty, and by six o'clock they were in their classrooms, warming up. And by lunchtime, she was one of them. Madame Markova had come to check on her several times, and watched her in her classes each day. She wanted to keep a close eye on her formation, and make sure that she was learning properly before she even began to dance. She saw immediately that the little bird that had flown to them from Moscow was a remarkably graceful child with the perfect body for a dancer. She was perfect for the life her father had chosen for her. And it was clear to Madame Markova, and her other teachers, in a short time, that destiny had brought her here. Danina Petroskova had been born to be a dancer.

As Madame Markova had promised from the first, Danina's life was one of rigor, backbreaking hard work, and sacrifices that demanded more from her each day than she thought possible. But in the first three years she was there, she never wavered or faltered in her determination. She was ten by then, and lived only to dance, and strove constantly for perfection. Her days were fourteen hours long, spent almost entirely in classes. She was tireless, always determined to surpass what she had previously learned. Madame Markova was well pleased with her, as she told Danina's father whenever she saw him. He came to see Danina several times a year, and was always pleased with what he saw of her dancing, as were her teachers.

When he came to see her first major performance on the stage, when she was fourteen, she danced the role of the girl who dances the mazurka with Franz in *Coppelia*. She was a full member of the troupe by then, and no longer merely a student, which pleased her father greatly. It was a beautiful performance, and Danina was breathtaking in her precision, elegance of style, and the sheer power of her talent. There were tears in her father's eyes when he saw her, and in hers when she saw him backstage after the performance. It was the most exciting night of her life, and all she wanted to do was thank him for bringing her here seven years before. She had lived at the ballet for half her life now, it was the only life she knew, the only one she wanted.

She danced the role of the Lilac Fairy in *Sleeping Beauty* a year later, and at sixteen, she gave a miraculous performance in *La Bayadère*. At seventeen, she was a prima and performed so breathtakingly in *Swan*

*Lake* that no one who saw her could forget it. Madame Markova knew that she lacked maturity in some ways, she had seen so little of the world, knew nothing of life, yet her technique and her style were so extraordinary that they took one's breath away, and put her far above the others.

The Czarina was well aware of her by then, as were her daughters. And at nineteen, Danina danced at a private performance for the Czar at the Winter Palace. It was April 1914. In May, she was invited to dance for them at their villa on the Peterhof estate, and dined with the family in their private quarters, with Madame Markova and several stars of the ballet in attendance. It was a treat for her, beyond any she had known, and a tribute that meant more to her than any other. To be recognized by the Czar and Czarina was the ultimate accolade, the only tribute she had truly longed for, and she put a photograph of them in a small frame next to her bed. She had particularly liked meeting Grand Duchess Olga, as she was only a few months younger than Danina. And Danina was enchanted by the

Czarevitch, who was only nine then, but he thought Danina was very pretty, as did everyone who saw her.

As she matured, Danina had a rare graceful quality, a sense of gentleness and poise, a bit of mischief, and a lovely sense of humor. It was not surprising that the Czarevitch loved her. He was delicate, and had been ill throughout his childhood. But despite his fragility, she teased him and treated him normally, and he loved it. He was a particularly wise, soulful child, and spoke longingly of what she did. She seemed so strong to him, so healthy.

Danina promised to let Alexei watch her in class one day, if Madame Markova would let them, but she couldn't imagine Madame Markova saying no to such an important visitor, if his health would permit it, and his doctors. Because of his hemophilia there was always one of two physicians hovering near, making sure no accident befell him. Danina felt sorry for him, he seemed so ill, and so intolerably frail, and yet there was something warm and kind and very loving about him. And the Czarina was very

touched when she saw how kind Danina
was to him.

As a result, that summer, Madame
Markova received an invitation from the
Czarina to come to stay at Livadia for a
week, their summer palace in the Crimea,
and to bring Danina with her. It was an
enormous honor, but even then, Danina
was reluctant to do it. She couldn't bear the
thought of abandoning her classes and rehearsals for seven days. She was conscien-
tious to the point of being driven. Hers was
a rigid, grueling, brutally demanding mo-
nastic life, which required everything of her.
She gave it everything she had, everything
she could, all she dared, and she had long
since far exceeded even Madame Markova's wildest dreams for her. It took Madame Markova nearly a month to convince
her to accept the Imperial invitation, and
only then because the ballet mistress convinced her that it would be an affront to the
Czarina if she didn't.

It was the only vacation she had ever
had, the only time in her life, since the age
of seven, when she hadn't been dancing,

when she didn't begin each day with warm-ups at five, classes at six, and rehearsals by eleven, when she didn't push her body for fourteen hours a day to its outer limits. At Livadia, in July, it was the first time in her life that she dared to play, and in spite of herself, she loved it.

Danina seemed almost childlike to Madame Markova as she watched her. She played with the Czar's daughters in the sea, cavorted with them, laughing and splashing, and was always gentle with Alexei. She had a motherly touch with him, which touched his mother's heart deeply. And all of the children were startled to realize that Danina didn't know how to swim. With all her discipline and the agonizingly stern life she led, she had never had time to learn anything but dancing.

It was on her fifth day there that Alexei fell ill again, after a small bump he had gotten on his leg while leaving the dinner table, and he was confined to his bed for the next two days. Danina sat with him, telling him stories she remembered from her childhood with her father and brothers, and endless tales of the ballet, the rigorous discipline, and the other dancers. He listened to her for hours, until he fell asleep holding her hand, and she tiptoed slowly away to rejoin the others. She felt so sorry for him, and the cruel limitations his illness imposed on him. He was so unlike her own brothers, or the boys she had trained with at the ballet, who were all so powerful and so healthy.

Alexei was still weak but feeling better when she and Madame Markova left in mid-July, and boarded the Imperial train to return to St. Petersburg. It had been a wonderful vacation, and an unforgettable time in her life that she knew she would remember forever. She would never forget playing with the Imperial family like ordinary friends, and the beauty of the setting, and Alexei trying to teach her to swim, while explaining it to her from a deck chair.

"No, not like that, you silly girl . . . like this. . . ." He demonstrated the strokes with his arms, while she tried to implement them, and then they both laughed hysterically when she failed and pretended to be drowning.

He wrote to her once at the ballet, a little note, telling her that he missed her. It was obvious that although he was only nine, he had a crush on her. His mother acknowledged it to a friend, with genteel amusement. Alexei was having his first affair with a ballet dancer, at nine, and she was a beauty. But better than that, they knew she was a lovely person. But two weeks after her idyllic stay in Livadia, the entire world was in turmoil, and the sad events in Sarajevo had finally catapulted them into war. And on August first, Germany declared war on Russia. No one thought it would last long, and optimistically assumed the hostilities would end at the Battle of Tannenberg at the end of August, but instead the situation worsened.

Despite the war, Danina danced in *Giselle* and *Coppelia* and *La Bayadère* again that year. Her skill was reaching its peak, and her development and understanding were all that Madame Markova had hoped they would be one day. There was never the slightest element of disappointment in her performance, it was everything it should have been, and more. What she brought to the stage was precisely what Madame Markova had sensed she might, years before.

And she had the kind of single-minded dedication and purpose that was essential. Danina allowed for no distractions from what she did. She cared nothing about men, or the world outside the walls of the ballet. She lived and breathed and worked and existed only for dancing. She was the perfect dancer, unlike some of the others, whom Madame Markova viewed with disdain. Despite their impeccable training and whatever talent they had, too often they allowed themselves to be distracted or lured away by men and romance. But to Danina, the ballet was her lifeblood, the force that drove and fed her. It was the very essence of her soul. For Danina, there was nothing else. It was everything she cared about, and lived for. And as a result, her dancing was exquisite.

She gave her best performance that year on Christmas Eve. Her brothers and father were at the front, but the Czar and Czarina were there, and were overwhelmed by the beauty of her dancing. She joined them in their box briefly afterward and asked immediately after Alexei. She gave his mother one of the roses that had been given her, and sent it to him, and Madame Markova noticed that she looked more tired than usual when she returned backstage. It had been a long, exciting evening, and Danina wouldn't have admitted it, but she felt exhausted.

She got up at five the next day, as usual, although it was Christmas Day, and was in the studio warming up by five-thirty. There was no class until noon that day, but she could never bear the idea of missing an entire morning. She was always afraid she would lose some part of her skill, if she wasted half a day, or even let herself be pulled away from it for a minute. Even on Christmas.

Madame Markova saw Danina in the studio at seven, and after watching her for a little while, she thought her exercises looked strange. There was a stiffness that was uncharacteristic of her, an awkwardness as she practiced her arabesques, and then very slowly, as though in slow motion, she began to drift toward the floor. Her movements were so graceful that as she fell, it looked rehearsed and absolutely perfect. It was only when she lay there, without moving, for what seemed like an eternity, that Madame Markova and two of the other students suddenly realized that she was unconscious. They ran to her immediately, and attempted to revive her, and Madame Markova knelt beside her on the floor. Her hands were trembling as she touched Danina's face and back, and felt the dry, blazing heat of her body. And as Danina opened unseeing eyes, her mentor saw instantly that they were feverish and glazed, and she had been devoured, during the night, by some mysterious illness.

"My child, why did you dance today if you are ill . . . ?" Madame Markova was beside herself as she looked at her. They had all heard of the raging influenza running unchecked through Moscow, but thus far there had been no sign of it in St. Petersburg. "You shouldn't have done this," Madame Markova scolded her gently, fearing the worst for her. But at first, Danina seemed almost not to hear her.

"I had to. . . . I had to. . . ." Missing a moment, a single exercise or class or rehearsal was more than Danina could bear. "I must get up. . . . I must . . ." she said, and then began to babble. One of the young men who had danced with her for a decade lifted her easily, and at Madame Markova's direction carried her to her bed upstairs. She had finally left the large dormitory the year before, and was now sleeping in a room with only six beds in it. It was as spartan and spare and icy cold as the dormitory where she had lived for eleven years, but it was a little bit more private, and now the other dancers came rapidly to hover in the doorway and watch her. News of her collapse had already spread everywhere, in all the halls of the ballet.

"Is she all right . . . what happened . . . she is so pale, Madame . . . what will happen . . . we must call a doctor. . . ." Danina herself was too tired to explain, too dazed to even recognize anyone. All she could see in the distance was the tall, spare form of Madame Markova, whom she loved as a mother, standing anxiously at the foot of her bed. But she was too tired to listen to what she was saying.

Madame Markova ordered everyone from the room, for fear of contagion to them, and asked one of the other teachers to bring some tea for Danina. But when Madame Markova put the cup to Danina's lips, she could not even sip it. Danina was far too ill, and much too weak. And just sitting up, with Madame Markova's powerful arms supporting her, she nearly fainted. She had never felt so ill in her life, but it no longer mattered to her. By that afternoon, when the doctor came, she knew she was going to die, and she didn't mind it. Every inch of her body ached, her limbs felt as though they had been severed with axes. Each touch, each movement, each brush against the rough sheets on her bed made her feel as though her skin were on fire. And all she could think of as she lay there, hovering between delirium and pain, was that if she did not exercise soon, and return to classes and rehearsal, she would die.

The doctor who came confirmed Madame Markova's earlier fears, and did little to allay her terror for Danina. It was indeed influenza, and he admitted honestly to the mistress of the ballet that there was nothing he could do about it. People had been dying in Moscow by the hundreds. And Madame Markova cried as she listened. She tried to urge Danina to be strong, but Danina had begun to sense that she would not win the battle, which terrified her mentor even further.

"Is it like Mama . . . do I have typhoid?" she whispered, too weak to speak aloud, or even to reach out and touch Madame Markova standing near her.

"Of course not, my child. It's nothing," she lied. "You have been working too hard. That's all. You must rest for a few days, and you'll be fine." But Madame Markova's words fooled no one, least of all the patient, who even in her groggy state was well aware of how ill she was, how hopeless the situation.

"I'm dying," she said quietly later that night, and she said it with such calm conviction that the teacher sitting with her ran to get Madame Markova. Both women were crying when they returned, but Madame Markova dried her eyes before coming to sit next to Danina again. She held a glass of water to the girl's lips, but was unable to convince her to take it. Danina had neither the desire, nor the strength, to drink. Her fever was still blazing, her eyes looked ill and wild. "I'm dying, aren't I?" she whispered to her old friend.

"I won't let you do that," Madame Markova said quietly. "You have not danced *Raimonda* yet, and I was planning to let you do that this year. It would be a shame to die without having at least tried that." Danina tried to smile but failed. She felt much too ill to answer.

"I can't miss rehearsal tomorrow," Danina croaked at her a little while later, as Madame Markova sat with her through the night. It was as though Danina felt that if she didn't dance, she might well die. The ballet was her life-force.

The doctor returned to see her again that morning, he applied several poultices, and gave her several drops of a bitter tasting liquid to drink, but to no avail. By late that afternoon, she was much worse. She was completely delirious that night, shouting unintelligibly and muttering darkly, and then laughing at people she imagined she saw, or things she heard but no one else did. It was an endless night for everyone, and in the morning Danina looked ravaged. The fever was so high that it was hard to imagine she had survived it this far, impossible to believe it would not kill her.

"We must do something," Madame Markova said, looking distracted. The doctor had insisted there was nothing more he could do, and she believed him, but perhaps another doctor would think of something else he hadn't. With a sense of desperation, Madame Markova jotted off a note in haste that afternoon to the Czarina, explaining the situation to her, and daring to ask if she had any suggestions, or knew someone they could call for Danina. Madame Markova knew, as everyone did, that there was a hospital set up in part of the Catherine Palace at Tsarskoe Selo, where the Czarina and Grand Duchesses nursed the soldiers. Perhaps there was someone there who would have some idea how to help Danina. Madame Markova was desperate by then, and willing to try anything to save her. Some people had survived the rampaging influenza in Moscow, but it seemed to be more a matter of luck, rather than anything more scientific.

The Czarina did not waste her time writing a response and immediately sent the

younger of the Czarevitch's two doctors to
Danina. The elder, the venerable Dr. Botkin, was himself felled at the time with a
bout of mild influenza. But Dr. Nikolai
Obrajensky, whom Danina had met that
summer in Livadia, was at the ballet school,
asking for Madame Markova long before
dinner. And she was greatly relieved to see
him, and murmured anxiously about the
kindness of the Czarina when she met him.
She was still so upset over Danina's condition at the time that she scarcely noticed
how much he resembled the Czar, though
in a somewhat younger version.

"How is she?" the doctor asked gently.
He could see from the state of Madame
Markova's distress that the young ballerina
must be no better. But even he, having seen
severe cases of influenza at the hospital,
had not expected to find the young dancer
so ill, or so worn by the illness that seemed
to have ravaged her nearly totally in the two
days she'd had it. She was dehydrated, delirious, and when he took her temperature,
he checked it again, unable to believe it was
as high as the thermometer said. He had
little hope for her survival after he read it

again, and examined her carefully, and he finally turned to Madame Markova with a dismal expression. "I'm afraid you already know what I am going to say . . . don't you?" he said, looking deeply sympathetic. He could see, from the woman's eyes, how much she loved Danina. She was like a daughter to her.

"Please . . . I can't bear it . . ." she said, dropping her face into her hands, too exhausted and strained herself to tolerate the blow he was about to deal her. "She's so young . . . so talented . . . she's only nineteen . . . she must *not* die. You must not let her," she said fiercely, looking up at him again, wanting something from him he could not give her. Hope, if not assurance.

"I cannot help her," he said honestly. "She would not even survive the trip to the hospital. Perhaps if she is still with us in a few days, we can move her." But he thought it less than likely, and Madame Markova knew that. "All you can do is try to keep her cool to bring the fever down, bathe her with cool cloths, and force her to drink as much as you can. The rest is in God's hands, Madame. Perhaps He needs her more than we do." His tone was kind, but he could not lie to her. He was only amazed that she had survived this long. He knew that some had died on the day the dreaded influenza felled them. And she had had it for two days now. "Do what you can for her, but know that you cannot work miracles, Madame. We can only pray now, and hope that He listens," Dr. Obrajensky said somberly. He had no hope for Danina.

"I understand," she said bleakly.

He sat with them for a while, and took her temperature again. It had risen slightly, and Madame Markova was already applying the cool cloths he had recommended. The students were bringing them to her, and keeping them damp and cool, but she would not let them in the room with her, for fear that they would get it. The five girls who normally occupied the room with her had been sent to the main dormitory to sleep on cots or on mattresses with the others. Their room was completely off-limits to them.

"How is she now?" Madame Markova asked him anxiously after she had been bathing Danina's chest and arms and face with cool cloths for an hour. The patient was completely unaware of their presence or attention, as she lay deathly pale and trembling, her face as white as the sheets she lay on.

"She is about the same," he answered when he checked her again. He didn't want to tell Madame Markova that he thought she was even a trifle warmer. "She will not improve so quickly." If ever, which he doubted. But even he was struck by how lovely Danina was as she lay lifelessly before them. She was a striking beauty, her features exquisitely delicate, her body minute and incredibly graceful. Her long dark brown hair was fanned out behind her on the pillow. But she had the look of someone near death, he knew only too well, and he was sure by then that she would not live till morning.

"Is there nothing more we can do?" Madame Markova asked, looking desperate.

"Pray," he said, and meant it. "Have you called her parents?"

"She has a father and four brothers. I believe that all are at the front, from what she has told me." The war had broken out only months before, and their regiment had been among the first to go. Danina was very proud of them, and mentioned it often.

"Then there is nothing you can do. We must wait and see." He looked at his watch then. He had been with Danina for three hours, and knew he should get back to Tsarskoe Selo to see about Alexei, and it would take him an hour to get there. "I will come back in the morning," he promised. But he feared that by then the good Lord would have taken matters into His own hands. "Send word to me if you feel you need me." He gave her the directions to his home, should they need to send someone for him. But by the time he came back with the person they sent, it might be too late for Danina. He lived beyond Tsarkoe Selo, with his wife and two children. He was still young, in his late thirties, but extremely responsible, capable and compassionate, which was why he had been entrusted with the care of the Czarevitch. And he looked oddly like the boy's father. He had the same distinguished features, was as tall as the Czar, and wore his beard in precisely the same neat, trim way the Czar did. Even without the beard, the doctor looked oddly like him, except that his hair was darker, almost the same color as Danina's.

"Thank you for coming, Dr. Obrajensky," Madame Markova said politely as she walked to the main door with him. It was a long walk, which took her far from her patient, but walking down the cool halls was a relief, and as she opened the heavy front door, a gust of cold air both startled and refreshed her.

"I wish there was more I could do for her . . . and for you . . ." he said kindly. "I can see how distressing this is for you."

"She is like my own child," Madame Markova said with tears filling her eyes, and he gently touched her arm at the sight of her sorrow. He felt utterly helpless.

"Perhaps God will be merciful and spare her." She could only nod then, bereft of words in the face of her emotions. "I will come back very early tomorrow morning."

"She begins warming up every day at five or five-thirty," Madame Markova said, as though it still mattered, but they both knew it didn't.

"She must work very hard. She is an extraordinary dancer," he said admiringly, unable to believe either of them would see her dance again, but happy that he had at least once. It seemed tragic to contemplate now.

"Have you seen her dance?" Madame Markova asked with mournful eyes.

"Only once. *Giselle.* It was lovely," he said kindly. He knew how hard this was for Madame Markova. It was easy to see it.

"She is even better in *Swan Lake,* and *Sleeping Beauty,*" she said with a sad smile.

"I will look forward to it," he said politely, bowed, and then left as she closed the heavy door behind him, and walked quickly through the halls to return to Danina.

It was an unforgettable night for Madame Markova, of sorrow and despair, and also fever, delirium, and terror for Danina. And finally, by morning, Danina seemed almost to have left them. Madame Markova was sitting at her bedside, looking lifeless herself, exhausted, but not daring to leave her even for an instant, when the doctor returned at five the next morning.

"Thank you for coming so early," she

whispered in the dismal room. The atmosphere was already one of loss and mourning. It seemed, even to her, impossible to win the fight now. Danina had not regained consciousness since the previous morning.

"I was worried about her all night," the doctor admitted, looking troubled. He could see from the older woman's face how the night had gone, and Danina was barely breathing. He checked her pulse and took her temperature, and was surprised to find her temperature a little lower, but her pulse was thin and thready. "She is putting up a good fight. We're lucky she is young and strong." But even the young had been dying in shocking numbers in Moscow, particularly children. "Has she taken any water?"

"Not in several hours," Madame Markova admitted. "I can't seem to get her to swallow, and I was afraid to choke her." He nodded. There was truly nothing they could do now, but he had arranged to stay for several hours. His senior colleague, Dr. Botkin, had improved sufficiently to be able to attend to the Czarevitch if he had to. Dr. Obrajensky wanted to be with Danina if she died, if only to offer comfort to her mentor.

They sat quietly side by side for hours, on hard chairs in the barren room, speaking little, and checking her from time to time. He suggested that Madame Markova try and get some rest while he was there, but she refused to leave her beloved ballerina.

It was noon when Danina finally made an anguished sound, and stirred uncomfortably. She sounded as though she was in pain, but as the doctor checked her again, he found nothing new or different in her condition. He could only marvel that she had hung on this long. It was a real tribute to her youth, her strength, and her physical condition. And remarkably, thus far, no one else in the ballet had caught it. Only Danina.

At four o'clock that afternoon, Dr. Obrajensky was still there, not wanting to abandon them before the end. Madame Markova had dozed off in her chair, and the doctor saw Danina become restless. She was moaning again, and stirring uncomfortably, but Madame Markova was too exhausted to hear her. The doctor examined her, and found her heart weak and irregular when he checked her. He was sure it was a sign that the end was near. Her pulse was rough as well, and she began having trouble breathing, all signs that he had been expecting. He would have liked to ease the end for her, but there was nothing he could do, except be there. He took her hand in his own, after taking her pulse again, and just stroked it gently, watching her, seeing the lovely young face so ill and so tormented. It hurt him to see it, and to be of so little use to her. It was like wrestling with demons, trying to win her. He wanted to will her back to life, to health. And he gently touched her forehead with his hand. She stirred again and said something. She sounded as though she were saying something to a friend, or one of her brothers. And then she said a single word and opened her eyes and looked at him. He had seen it a hundred times, it was a last surge of life before the end. Her eyes were wide open then, as she spoke clearly and said, "Mama, I see you."

"It's all right, Danina, I'm here," he said soothingly. "Everything is going to be all right now." Very soon, it would be over.

"Who are you?" she said in a hoarse,

ragged voice, as though she could see him clearly, but he knew she couldn't. She was seeing someone in her delirium, but it was unlikely it was the doctor she was seeing.

"I'm your doctor," he said quietly. "I came here to help you."

"Oh," she said, and closed her eyes again, laying her head back against the pillow. "I'm going to see my mother." He remembered then what Madame Markova had said about her only having a father and brothers, and he understood what she meant, but he wouldn't let her continue.

"I don't want you to do that," he said firmly. "I want you to stay here with me. We need you, Danina."

"No, I must go . . ." she said with her eyes closed, turning her head away from him. "I'll be late for class, and Madame Markova will be angry at me." It was the most she had said in two days, and it was clear that she wanted to leave them, or knew she had to.

"You must stay for class here, Danina . . . or Madame Markova and I will both be very angry. Open your eyes, Danina . . . open your eyes and see me."

And much to his surprise, she did, and looked right at him with enormous eyes in the small, pale face that seemed to have shrunk with the fever.

"Who are you?" she said again, this time in a voice that sounded as ravaged as she felt, as damaged as she had been, and this time he knew she could see him. He touched her forehead gently, and for the first time in two days, it was markedly cooler.

"I am Nikolai Obrajensky, mademoiselle. I am your doctor. The Czarina sent me."

She nodded then and closed her eyes again for a moment, and then opened them again to say something to him in a whisper. "I saw you with Alexei last summer . . . in Livadia. . . ." She remembered. She had returned. She still had a long way to go, but incredible as it seemed, perhaps finally the spell had been broken. He wanted to shout with excitement, but he didn't want to celebrate too soon. It could still be the burst of energy before the end. He did not yet trust what he was seeing.

"I will teach you how to swim this sum-

mer if you stay here," he teased gently, remembering the fun they'd all had when
Alexei tried to teach her. She almost
smiled, but she still felt far too ill to be able
to do more than look at him weakly.

"I have to dance," she said, sounding
worried. "I don't have time to swim. . . ."

"Yes, you do. You are going to have to
rest for a while now." She opened her eyes
wide as he said it, and he felt encouraged
again. She was entirely cognizant of what he
was saying.

"I have to go to class tomorrow."

"I think you should go this afternoon,"
he teased her, and this time she smiled,
though it was barely more than a rictus.
"You're being very lazy." He was smiling at
her now, feeling as though he had won the
battle of a lifetime. He had had no hope at
all for this one. An hour before, she had
been all but gone, and now she was awake
and talking to him.

"I think you're being very silly," she
whispered. "I can't go to class today."

"Why not?"

"No legs," she said, looking worried.
"Fell off, I think, can't feel them." He

looked worried then, and reached under the covers to touch her legs, and he asked her what she felt when he touched her. She felt everything, she was just too weak to move them.

"You're just weak, Danina," he reassured her. "You are going to be fine now." But he also knew that if in fact she did survive, and it looked at least remotely possible, though she was not yet out of the woods completely, her recovery would take months, and she would have to be carefully and expertly nursed, if she was to recover completely. "You're going to have to be very good, and sleep a great deal, and eat and drink," and as though to prove it to her, he offered her a sip of water, and this time she took it. She only took one sip, but it was a vast improvement. And as he set the glass down on the table next to her, Madame Markova woke with a start, afraid that something terrible had happened while she was sleeping. But instead, she saw Danina looking weak but alive again, smiling wanly up at the doctor.

"My God, it's a miracle," she said, fighting back tears of relief and exhaustion.

She looked almost as bad as Danina, but she had no fever and was not ill. She was simply devastated by the terror of nearly losing Danina. "Child, are you feeling better?"

"A little." Danina nodded, and then glanced up again at the doctor. "I think you saved me."

"No, I didn't. I wish I could take credit for it, but I'm afraid I've been quite useless. All I did was sit here. Madame Markova did a great deal more for you than I did."

"God did it," Madame Markova said firmly, "and your own strength." She wanted desperately to ask the doctor if she'd be all right now, but she knew she couldn't ask him in front of the patient. But Danina certainly seemed much better. She seemed alert, and stronger, and as though she had turned the corner. They had come so close to losing her that Madame Markova was still shaking.

"How soon can I dance again?" she asked him, and both the doctor and Madame Markova laughed. She was indeed feeling better.

"Not next week, I can promise you

that, my friend." He smiled as he said it. Not for months, but he knew it was too soon to say it to her. He could sense easily that if he told her the truth, she would grow frantic with guilt and worry. "Soon. If you're a good girl, and do everything I tell you to, you'll be up on your feet again in no time."

"I have an important rehearsal tomorrow," she insisted.

"I think there's a good chance you might miss it. No legs, remember?"

"What was that?" Madame Markova looked worried by his comment, but he was quick to explain it.

"She couldn't feel her legs a minute ago, but they're fine. She's just very weak from the fever." And a moment later when they tried to sit her up for another drink, they found she couldn't even do that much. She could barely get her head up off the pillow.

"I feel like a piece of string," she said eloquently, and he laughed softly at her.

"You look a bit better than that. Much better, in fact, I think I might go back to my other patients before they forget what I look like." It was after six o'clock, and he had been with her for thirteen hours, but he promised to return again the next morning. And as they walked to the front door, Madame Markova thanked him profusely and asked what to expect now.

"A long, long recovery," he said honestly. "She must spend at least a month in bed, or she will risk getting sick again, and the next time she may not be as lucky." The mere thought of it filled Madame Markova with horror. "It will be many months before she can dance again. Three, maybe four. Perhaps longer."

"We'll tie her down if we have to. You heard what she's like. She'll be begging to dance by tomorrow morning."

"She'll be surprised herself by how weak she is. She'll have to be patient, it will take time now."

"I understand," Madame Markova said gratefully, and thanked him again before he left. And after she closed the door behind him, she walked slowly back to Danina's room, thinking how devastating it would have been if she had died, and how lucky they had all been not to lose her. She was infinitely grateful to the Czarina, too, for sending them her doctor. There had been little he could do, but just having him there had been an enormous comfort. And he had been remarkably dedicated, staying as long as he had with Danina.

And as Madame Markova walked back into Danina's room, she looked at the young woman she loved so much, and smiled. Danina lay in her bed, looking like a child. There was a small smile on her lips, and she was sleeping.

# Chapter 2

*T*rue to his word, Dr. Obrajensky came to see Danina again the next day, but this time he did not come until the afternoon because he knew she was out of danger. And he was pleased to see, when he returned, that she was eating and drinking. She still barely had the strength to lift her head off the pillow, but she smiled as soon as he entered the room. She was obviously happy to see him.

"How is Alexei?" she asked the moment she saw him.

"Very well indeed. Far better than you now. He was playing cards and beating his sister soundly at it when I saw him this morning. He said to tell you he hopes you feel better soon, as did all the Grand Duchesses, and the Czarina."

In fact, she had sent a note to Madame Markova, and Dr. Obrajensky knew what was in it. The Czarina had asked his advice in the matter.

Madame Markova was still in the sickroom with her, but even she was looking considerably more rested. And when she read the note from the Czarina, her eyes widened and she looked startled. She looked up at him in surprise, and he nodded. It had been his suggestion. The Czarina had invited Danina to come and stay in one of their guest cottages for her convalescence. She could be well cared for there, and make the long recovery she would need, without tormenting herself by being right in the midst of the ballet. Being in Tsarskoe Selo would be restful for her, she could be well supervised, and well nursed, and convalesce in just the way she needed, to make a full recovery and return to the ballet.

After they left Danina's room that afternoon, the doctor asked Madame Markova what she thought of the Czarina's invitation. She was still more than a little startled. It was an extremely flattering invitation, but she had no idea how Danina would feel about accepting. She was so tightly woven into the ballet, Madame Markova couldn't imagine her wanting to leave it for a minute, even if she could not dance now. Though admittedly, being there and watching them, and not being able to dance with them for months, would eventually drive her crazy.

"It might be very good for her to get away," Madame Markova admitted, "but I'm not sure we can convince her of that. Even if she can't dance, I suspect she will want to stay. She hasn't left us in twelve years, except last summer for her visit to Livadia."

"But she liked that, didn't she? This would be more of the same. And besides, I can keep an eye on her there. It's hard for me to get away as often and for as long as I have in the last few days. I have my responsibilities to the Czarevitch."

"You've been very kind to her," Madame Markova admitted freely. "I don't know what we'd have done without you."

"I did absolutely nothing to help her," he said modestly, "except pray, just as you did. She has been very lucky." As much in the support of the Imperial family as in the attentions of their doctor. "I think the Czarina, and the children, will be very disappointed if she doesn't come." And then he reminded Madame Markova gently of what she already knew. "It is a very unusual invitation. I think Danina would really enjoy it."

"Who wouldn't?" Madame Markova laughed honestly. "I have at least a dozen ballerinas, if not more, who would be more than happy to take her place at Tsarskoe Selo. The problem is, Danina is different. She never wants to leave here, she's afraid she might miss something. She never goes to shops, or out for walks, or to the theater. She dances, and she dances . . . and she dances, and then she watches the others dance, and dances some more. Besides, she is very attached to me. Probably because she has no mother." And it was obvious that Madame Markova genuinely loved her.

"How long has she been here?" he

asked with interest. He was fascinated by her, she was like a rare, delicate bird who had landed at his feet with a broken wing, and now he wanted to do everything he could to help her. Even intercede on her behalf with the Czar and Czarina. But it was not a difficult task, they also admired and liked her. It was impossible not to admire someone with so vast a talent.

"She has been here for twelve years," Madame Markova answered his question. "Since she was seven. She is nineteen now, nearly twenty."

"Perhaps a little holiday will do her good." He was being very firm about it. He thought it was important for her.

"I agree. The problem is convincing her. I'll talk to her about it when she's a little stronger."

He came every day after that, and a few days later, Madame Markova broached the subject with her. Danina was startled at first at the invitation from the Imperial family, and pleased, but she had no intention of accepting. "I can't leave you," she said simply to Madame Markova. She herself was unnerved by her brush with death, and the ballet was home to her. She didn't want to recuperate among strangers, even royal ones. "You won't make me go, will you?" she asked, looking worried.

But as soon as they tried to get her up, she realized the full impact of her illness, as did Madame Markova. She couldn't even sit in a chair without nearly fainting and being held there for her own safety. And she had to be carried to the bathroom.

"You need constant nursing," the doctor explained to her on one of his visits, "and you will for a while, Danina. It will be a tremendous burden for the people here. They are all really much too busy to help you." She knew it was the truth, and what a burden she'd been to everyone already, especially Madame Markova. But she still didn't want to leave them. This was her home, and they were her family. She couldn't bear the thought of leaving, and she cried that night when she and Madame Markova talked about it.

"Why can't you go for a little while?" Madame Markova suggested. "Just until

you're a bit stronger. It is such a kind invitation, and you really might enjoy it."

"It frightens me," she said simply. But
the next morning Madame Markova insisted that Danina accept the offer. Aside
from thinking it would do Danina good, she
was afraid to offend the Czarina by not accepting her generous invitation. It was rare,
if not unheard of, to be invited to convalesce at Tsarskoe Selo, and she was very
grateful to Dr. Obrajensky for having arranged it. He had proven to be not only
kind, but inordinately thoughtful, and genuinely concerned with Danina. And his daily
visits had done wonders to cheer her. Spiri-
tually at least, she was nearly herself now. It
was her body that was not willing, or able,
to bounce back as quickly.

"I think you should go," Madame Markova said firmly. And then finally, by the
end of the week, she and the doctor came
to an agreement. Danina must be sent,
whether or not she wanted to go. It was for
her own good. Without proper nursing, she
might never recover completely, and never
be able to dance again. And finally, Ma-

dame Markova said as much to Danina. "What if your stubbornness costs you the ballet forever?" she said sternly.

"Do you think that might happen?" Danina's eyes were filled with terror.

"It could," Madame Markova said, looking worried. "You were very, very ill, my dear. You must not tempt fate now by being stubborn or foolish." They had invited her to stay indefinitely, until she was well and able to return to the ballet again. It was an extraordinary invitation, and even Danina knew it. She was being childish, and didn't want to leave the security of familiar surroundings and the people she knew there.

"What if I go for a few weeks?" It was a small concession on her part, but at least a beginning.

"You will still not be able to dance then. At least go for a month, and we will see how you feel then. If you hate being there, you can always come back and continue convalescing here. But at least go for a month, you can always stay longer if you want to, since they have been kind enough to invite you. And I promise I will come and visit you."

It was a hard compromise for Danina, but she finally agreed. And the day she was to leave, she cried rivers at the thought of leaving her friends and mentor. "We're not sending you to Siberia," Madame Markova reminded her gently.

"It feels like it," Danina smiled through her tears, dismally sorry to leave them. "I will miss you so much," she said, clinging to Madame Markova's hand. A special covered sled had been sent for her journey. It was warm and comfortable and filled with furs and heavy blankets. The Czarina had spared nothing for her. And Dr. Obrajensky had come to accompany her. But before he came, he had checked everything for her in the guest house, which was warm and comfortable, and he knew she would be very happy in it. He also carried a message from Alexei, who could hardly wait to see her, and said he had a new card trick to teach her.

The dancers were all lined up outside to see her off, and everyone waved as the sled drove away, with the doctor sitting beside her. She was so nervous that he held her hand, and she waved frantically at them with the other. And before they even reached Tsarskoe Selo, she was exhausted from the emotions of the departure.

"It's my whole life, you know. I don't know anything else. I've been there for so long, I can't imagine being anywhere else, even for a minute." She explained it to him as they rode along, but he already understood it. And as always, he was kind and sympathetic.

"You're not going to lose anything by being away for a while. You'll get your strength back, Danina, just as you should, and they'll all be waiting for you when you return. And you'll be better than ever. Trust me." She did, and she was grateful for his support and companionship on the trip. It was so easy being with him. It was easy to see why the whole Imperial family loved him.

And as soon as they arrived, he settled her comfortably in the little guest house, which was more luxurious than anything she had ever dreamed. The bedroom was done all in pink satin, and the living room was a lovely blue and yellow. There were beautiful antiques everywhere, a kitchen to prepare her meals, there were four servants to take care of her, and two nurses. And half an hour after she arrived, the Czarina came to visit her, and brought Alexei with her, so he could show Danina his card trick. Both of them were shocked to see how hard hit she had been by her illness, and were glad that she had come there to recover. They only stayed a little while, so as not to tire her, and when they left, the doctor went with them. He didn't want to exhaust her either, and he promised to come and see her again in the morning to make sure she was "behaving."

It was odd for her, being there that night, without all the familiar people she knew, and the other girls she was accustomed to sleeping near. Despite the luxurious surroundings, she felt lonely. And she was surprised when the nurse came into her room, shortly after settling her in bed, and told her she had a visitor. Dr. Obrajensky had returned to see her. It was only eight o'clock, but she hadn't been expecting him again until morning, and she was surprised by the unexpected visit.

"I was on my way home," he explained, "and thought I'd come by to see how you were doing." He looked her over carefully from where he stood, and could see that his suspicions had been correct. She was looking a little mournful. "I had a feeling you might be lonely."

"I was," she confessed sheepishly, wondering how he knew. He seemed to understand so much about her. "I suppose that's silly of me." She was embarrassed to seem so ungrateful to him.

"Of course it's not," he said, pulling a chair up next to her bed, and sitting beside her. "You're accustomed to living in a community of people." He had seen the room she lived in with five other dancers, and had begun to know many of the others in the time he visited her after her illness. "It's a big change for you being all alone here." And she was still so young, only nineteen. She was so disciplined and mature in some ways, but extremely protected and childlike in others. And he loved that about her. "Is there anything I can do to make it easier for you?"

"No, I love your visits." She smiled at him. The one this evening had particularly touched her, because he seemed to understand exactly what she was feeling.

"Then I shall have to visit more often," he promised. It was easier for him to see her now, it was a short walk between her cottage and the Alexander Palace. He knew that Alexei and his sisters were already planning to keep her company, that was their intention, and the whole point of her coming. "You won't be lonely for long, and soon you can go for walks, and go over to the palace, when you're stronger." She still couldn't walk across the room without assistance. "I predict you will feel better in no time." She felt foolish suddenly for being lonely. Everyone was being so kind to her. In spite of missing her friends and Madame Markova, she was suddenly glad she had come here.

"Thank you for arranging it," she said gratefully. "I'm happy to be here."

"I'm glad you came, Danina," he said

quietly, looking relaxed and a little tired. It was the end of a long day for him, and she was sure he was anxious to get home to his wife and children. She felt guilty keeping him with her, but she enjoyed being with him. "I would have been so disappointed if you hadn't come."

"So would I," she admitted with a smile that touched deep into his heart, although she didn't know it. "This house is lovely." She looked around admiringly, still awed by the luxury they had lavished on her. She had never seen anything like it.

"I thought you'd like it." He smiled gently at her.

"It would be hard not to," she admitted.

"Will you miss dancing terribly?" he asked, already knowing the answer, but fascinated by her life at the ballet.

"I live to dance," she said. "It is the only life I know, the only one I want. I cannot imagine existing without it. Not being able to dance would probably kill me." He nodded, watching her eyes, her face. He loved talking to her. And now that she was feeling better, she had a delicious sense of humor.

"You'll dance again soon, Danina, I promise." But not too soon. She had a lot of ground to cover before she was strong enough to do that, and they both knew it. "You'll have to think of something else to do in the meantime." He had already brought a stack of books for her, and she had promised herself she would read them. She never had time to read anything when she was dancing.

"Do you like poetry?" he asked cautiously, not wanting to seem foolish and pedantic to her, but it was one of his passions.

"Very much." She nodded.

"I'll bring some tomorrow. I'm especially fond of the works of Pushkin. Perhaps you'd like him." She had read a little of him years before, and would be happy to read more of his work, since she had the time now. "I'll come and see you tomorrow after I see Alexei. Perhaps I can have lunch here, so you won't be too solitary." And with that, he stood up, but he seemed reluctant to leave her. "You'll be all right tonight, won't you?" He was worried about her, he didn't want her to be unhappy.

"I'll be fine," she said with a warm smile. "I promise. Now go home to your family or they'll think I'm a dreadful nuisance."

"They understand what it is to live with a doctor. I'll see you tomorrow then," he said from the doorway, and she waved from her bed, thinking again how kind he was and how lucky she was to know him.

# Chapter 3

*T*he book that Dr. Obrajensky brought the next day was so beautiful it brought tears to her eyes as he read some of it to her. He was slowly opening a door to a world she had never known or dreamed of, a world of intellectual pursuits and cerebral interests. Only that morning, she had begun reading one of the novels he had left her. And over lunch, they discussed it. Like the poetry he had brought, it was among his favorites. And the time she spent talking to him seemed to pass like minutes.

They were both surprised to discover that it was four o'clock in the afternoon when he left, and he hated to admit, she looked exhausted.

"I should not be the one tiring you," he

said, looking remorseful. "I of all people should know better."

"I'm fine," she promised him, having thoroughly enjoyed the time they spent talking. She had eaten lunch in bed, and he had sat at a small table near her.

"I want you to sleep now," he said gently, helping her settle deeper into her bed and rearranging her pillows for her. It was a job the nurse could do, but he liked doing it for her. "Sleep for as long as you can. I am dining at the palace tonight, and I'll check on you on my way home, if that's all right with you." It was what he had done the night before, and she had loved it. It had blown away the cobwebs of loneliness she had been feeling.

"I'd like that," she said, already looking sleepy. He turned off the lights next to her, and walked quietly out of the room, and turned to look at her from the doorway. Her eyes were already closed, and by the time he left the little house, she was sleeping. And she slept peacefully until dinner.

When she woke up she found a drawing next to her bed. Alexei had come to visit her that afternoon, and the nurse had told him she was sleeping. He had left a drawing for her, of her trying to swim the previous summer. Like most boys his age, he loved to tease her. And he felt particularly comfortable with her, as she was the same age as his sisters.

She had soup for dinner that night, and she was sipping tea when Dr. Obrajensky came back to see her on his way home from the Alexander Palace. He seemed to be in a lighthearted mood, and told her all about his dinner. He dined with the Imperial family several times a week, in fact more often than he did not.

"They are wonderful people," he said warmly. He was a great admirer of both the Czar and the Czarina. "They have so much responsibility, so many burdens. It's a hard time in the world, especially now with the war. And there has been a great deal of unrest in the cities. And of course, Alexei's health is always a great worry to them." His hemophilia was a constant problem, which necessitated the presence of a doctor near him at every instant. It was why the doctor spent as much time as he did with them, although he shared the responsibility with Dr. Botkin.

"It must be hard for you too," Danina said quietly, "having to be away from your family so much, and your own children." Danina knew that his wife was English and that they had two boys, twelve and four-teen.

"The Czar and Czarina seem to under-stand it, and they're very kind about inviting Marie. But she never comes. She hates so-cial occasions. She prefers to be at home with the boys, or just sitting quietly and sewing. She has no interest whatsoever in my work or the people I work for."

It was hard for Danina to believe, par-ticularly given who they were. They were hardly ordinary employers. And she couldn't help wondering if in some way his wife was jealous of him. It was hard to be-lieve she was that antisocial. Perhaps she was shy, or awkward in some way.

"Her Russian is poor, too, which makes it difficult for her. She's really never taken the time to learn it." It was a long-standing bone of contention between them, although he didn't say that to Danina. It would have seemed disloyal to complain about Marie to her, and yet it intrigued him that the two women seemed so different. The one so filled with vitality, the other so tired, so unhappy, so bored, so constantly disenchanted about something.

Even after her illness, Danina's energy and excitement about life was contagious. And her conversations with him were a new experience for her as well. Other than the boys she danced with at the ballet, she had never had men friends, been courted by anyone, or had a romance. Her only relationship with men had been with her brothers as a child, and now she seldom saw them anymore. They were always too busy to come to visit. They came to St. Petersburg to see her dance about once a year, and her father came scarcely more often. They were deeply involved with their responsibilities to the army.

But with Nikolai Obrajensky, it was all so different. He was becoming her friend, someone she could really talk to. She said so now, and he looked pleased to hear it. He loved talking to her, sharing his books and his views and the poetry he loved. In fact, there was a great deal he loved about her, and he also told himself that theirs was a comfortable friendship. He had almost mentioned her to Marie before she arrived, and had when she was very, very ill, but only in passing. He said he had been called to the ballet for one of the dancers who had a lethal case of influenza. But she had never asked him about it again, and once he knew Danina better, he had decided not to say anything more about her. In some ways, it was easier keeping their friendship a secret.

Years ago, he wouldn't have done that, but now, after fifteen years, he found that he had little or no desire to tell Marie about his life. She seemed completely uninterested in it. She had nothing to say to him most of the time. They had gone through a hard patch for a while, a few years before, when she wanted to go back to England. Or at least send their sons to school there. But he had objected to it. He wanted them close to him, where he could see them. But now she wasn't even angry about it. She was completely indifferent to him. But she never missed an opportunity to tell him how much she hated Russia, and living there. In contrast, the time he spent with Danina was so easy. She had no complaints about her life. She loved everything about it, and she was basically a happy person.

"Do your boys look like you?" she asked casually.

"People say they do." He smiled. "I don't really see it. I think they look more like their mother. They're fine children. They're actually growing up to be young men now. I think of them as little boys, and I have to remind myself they no longer are. They get very angry at me about it. They're very independent. They'll be men soon, and probably going off to the army to serve the Czar." Thinking about it reminded her of her brothers, and made her long for them. She worried about them a lot more now, ever since war had been declared the previous summer.

She told him about them then, and he smiled, listening. She was regaling him with tales of them, when she referred to him as "doctor," and he looked at her sadly. It made him feel so old, and distant from her, not the friends they had become in the short time they'd known each other.

Although she'd met him the previous summer at Livadia, it was only now, since she'd been ill, that she really came to know him. And their friendship was strong and growing.

"Can't you call me Nikolai?" he asked. "It seems much simpler somehow." And very personal, but she didn't think anything of it. She liked him. He asked it so humbly that, like so many other things he said, it touched her, and she smiled at him, looking more like a child than a young woman. Their friendship was so innocent and so harmless.

"Of course, if you prefer it. I can still address you more formally in front of others." It seemed more respectful, and she was sensitive both to his position and the difference in age between them. He was twenty years older than she was.

"That sounds reasonable." He seemed pleased with the agreement.

"Will I meet your wife while I'm here?"

Danina asked, curious about her, and his children.

"I doubt it," he said honestly. "She comes to the palace as little as possible. As I said, she hates going out, and declines all the Czarina's invitations, except perhaps once a year, when she feels obliged to."

"Will it hurt you with the Imperial family?" Danina asked openly. "Does the Czarina get angry about it?"

"Not that I'm aware of. If she does, she is far too discreet to say so. And I think she realizes that my wife is not an easy person." It was the first real glimpse she'd had into his home life. In truth, although they had spoken of many things, she knew nothing personal about him. And she had envisioned him with a warm family, and a happy home life.

"Your wife must be very shy," Danina said generously.

"No, I don't think so." He smiled sadly. Unlike Danina, there were so many differences between them. "She doesn't like wearing fancy clothes and evening gowns. She's very English. She likes to ride and to hunt, she likes being at her father's estate in Hampshire. And anything other than that is boring to her." He didn't say "including me," but he would have liked to, to Danina. For a long time now, their marriage had been a disappointment to both of them, but mainly to him, except for the existence of their children. But they were very different. She was cool and aloof, and indifferent in many ways. And he was warm and open. She was bored by the life he led, and in angry moments called him the Czar's lap-dog. And Nikolai was sick to death of her complaining about it. It was easy to under-stand why she had no friends here, she was so cold and so jealous. Even their sons were tired of her complaints. All she really wanted was to go back to England. And she expected him to drop everything, all his re-sponsibilities here, and come with her, which wasn't even remotely likely. If she ever went back permanently, he had warned her, she would have to do so without him.

"Why does she dislike it so much here?" Danina asked with open curiosity.

"The winters, or so she says. The weather is hardly more pleasant in England, although here it's colder. She doesn't like the people, or the country. She even hates the food." He smiled. It was an ancient litany between them.

"She'd like it better if she learned Russian," Danina said simply.

"I've tried to explain that to her. It's her way of not committing herself to staying here. As long as she doesn't speak Russian, she's not really here, or so she thinks. But it doesn't make life easy for her." It had been a long fifteen years for him, particularly for the past few years, but he didn't go so far as to explain all of that to Danina. Or how lonely he was. Or how glad he was to sit here talking to her, or share his books with her. If it wasn't for the boys, he would have let Marie go back to England years before. There was nothing between them now, except their children. "Her father is frightening her now about the war. And he thinks that one day there will be a revolution. He says the country is too big to control, and Nicholas is too weak to do it, which is ridiculous. But she believes that. Her father has always been something of a hysteric."

Danina listened with worried eyes. She

knew nothing about politics. She was normally much too busy dancing to know what
went on in the world. "Do you believe that
as well?" she asked solemnly. "About a
revolution?" She trusted his judgment completely.

"Not for a moment," Nikolai answered
her. "I don't think there is the remotest
chance of a revolution here. Russia is too
powerful for something like that to happen.
And so is the Czar. It's just another excuse
to complain about being here. She says I'm
risking the lives of our children. She's always been very influenced by her father."
He smiled at her then. She had such fresh
ideas, and such an open mind. She had
been exposed to so little, other than the ballet, that it was like watching her discover
the world around her. A world he found he
loved sharing with her. Compared to her,
Marie seemed so tired, and so angry, and so
bitter. Living in Russia had not improved
her disposition.

Marie had been pretty once, and interested in things. They had shared a lot of
common views and interests. She had been
fascinated by medicine, and his career. But

she resented his position in the Imperial family, and she seemed to resent a lot of things about him. But there was none of that in Danina. But then again, Marie was seventeen years older than Danina. He was thirty-nine, and his wife was three years his junior. Danina was still a baby. And she was relieved by what he had said about the revolution.

"Do you think the war will end soon?" she asked him innocently, and he smiled at her reassuringly, although the number of casualties and men lost to it thus far had been enormous. Everyone had expected it to end months ago, and to everyone's amazement, it hadn't.

"I hope so," he said simply.

"I worry about my father and brothers," she admitted to him.

"They'll be all right. We all will." Talking to him made her feel so much better. He sat with her for a long time and then finally he got up to leave. She looked tired again, and he had to get home. He couldn't avoid it forever. "I'll see you tomorrow," he promised her when he left, and she listened to his sled disappear into the darkness.

She was thinking about the things he had said about his wife, and the fact that he hadn't looked happy when he said them. He seemed to be trapped in a difficult situation, and she couldn't help wondering if there was anything he could do to improve it. Perhaps insist that his wife learn Russian, or travel back to England with her from time to time. It shocked her that she didn't seem to want to share his alliance with the Imperial family. It was hard to understand his wife's reactions. And then she found herself wondering if he was being unnecessarily gloomy about it. Maybe he was just tired, she thought to herself, as she lay in bed, thinking about him. The war was depressing everyone these days. Perhaps his comments about his wife were born of that, and other worries he hadn't mentioned.

It never occurred to her for an instant that he might want more from her, or have an interest in her other than as her doctor. He was married, after all, and he had a family. And even if he had some complaints about his wife, surely it wasn't as bad as it sounded. To Danina, looking at the world through the tiniest of telescopes, from her small world at the ballet, it all seemed very simple to her, and marriage was sacred. She was sure he was happier with Marie than he appeared or admitted.

For the next two weeks, he never mentioned his wife again when he came to visit her. She was able to dine at the table now, and on a sunny afternoon in January, he took her for a short walk in her garden. The air felt invigorating, and she was laughing with him, and teasing him about the fact that he took life so seriously. He had lent her volumes of poetry by then, and she had already read four of his favorite novels. And that afternoon when Alexei came to tea, Nikolai stayed and joined them. They played cards afterward, and Alexei won, much to his utter delight, and he squealed with glee when Danina accused him of cheating.

"I did not!" he said staunchly. "You played very badly, Danina." He said it matter-of-factly and she pretended to look outraged.

"How dare you! I played brilliantly. I'm

convinced that you cheated." Nikolai was enjoying watching them, and the good spirits between them.

"I did not cheat, and if you accuse me of it, when I'm Czar, I will remember it and have you beheaded."

"I don't think anyone does that anymore." Danina turned to Nikolai. "Do they?"

"If I want to, I will," Alexei announced, looking enchanted by the prospect. "And maybe I'll have your feet chopped off too, so you can't dance anymore, and your hands, so you can't play cards."

"I don't think I'll be able to do any of those things if you behead me, anyway. I think that ought to do it." Danina was smiling as she said it.

"Well, just in case, I'll chop off the rest." The prospect, to him, was deliciously gory. And then, out of the blue, he looked at her with interest. "Can I come and watch you dance one day in St. Petersburg? When you go back, I mean. I'd really like that."

"So would I," she said warmly.

"But I don't want you to go back for a long time. So not too soon," and then he remembered. "My mother said to ask you if you are well enough to come to dinner." He turned to Nikolai then. "Is she?"

"Maybe next week. It's a little soon still." She had only been there for two weeks, and was still somewhat unsteady on her feet, and tired quickly.

"I didn't bring anything to wear," she lamented.

"You can wear your nightgown," he said practically. "I'm sure no one will notice."

"How embarrassing." She laughed at the thought, but she really didn't have anything to wear for a dinner with the Imperial family.

"I'm sure one of the girls could lend you something," Alexei said politely. She was roughly the same size they were.

"Will you be there?" Danina asked Nikolai innocently, hoping he would be. She was so comfortable with him, it would be easier for her if he would be. Dining with the Imperial family still sounded more than a little daunting to her.

"Probably," he said, smiling at her. "I haven't heard anything about it yet, but if

I'm on duty that night, I'll be there." And he knew that even if they hadn't planned to include him, he could arrange it by adjusting the schedule so he would be on duty. Both physicians were pretty flexible about their schedules, and his colleague had more reason to go home at night than Nikolai, and was happy to let Nikolai work in the evenings.

Nikolai took Alexei back to the palace eventually, and Danina went to have a nap. And when she woke up, she was surprised to see Nikolai standing there in her bedroom, watching her, and he was frowning.

"Is something wrong?" She wondered if something had happened, there was a look in his eyes that worried her, but she didn't know what it meant. And he wasn't sure how to say it.

"I just wanted to check on you. I was worried that you walked too much this afternoon, considering it was your first time in the garden."

"I'm fine," she said, sitting up and looking at him. She was dying for some exercise, but she knew she wasn't up to it yet. It was very frustrating, and she wondered how long it would take to train herself again when she went back to the ballet. She was afraid that all of her muscles and ligaments would forget that she was a dancer. "I just slept for two hours. It was fun playing cards with Alexei."

"He does cheat, by the way. He always beats me," Nikolai said with a broad grin. "You had him pegged completely. And he loved it. He talked all the way home about beheading you, and how messy it would be, and how much he's going to enjoy it."

"I'm not sure that's very imperial behavior." She grinned at Nikolai, enjoying seeing him again, and wondering if he was on his way to dinner. She asked, and he said he was. It was his night on duty at the palace.

"I'll try and come over afterward, but it might be late, and I think you're probably tired today, after your walk in the garden." And as he said it, the nurse brought in her tray for dinner. She was making a very good recovery. She'd had a letter from Madame Markova that afternoon, who had told her not to rush back to the ballet. But she still felt incredibly guilty not to be dancing.

Madame Markova had given her all the news, and told her as well that one of the other girls had come down with influenza, but fortunately a mild case. She'd only been sick for two days and never even had a fever. She'd been far luckier than Danina.

The doctor lingered for a while, chatting with her, and then reluctantly left her for dinner at the palace. And as she sat quietly in bed, sipping her tea, she thought about him. He was a gentle man, with a warm, kind spirit, and she was grateful for his friendship. Were it not for him, and his intercession for her, she would not even have been there, in the guest cottage of the Czar, living in luxury, being pampered by servants and nurses. It was extraordinary to think how kind they had all been, and how lucky she was not only to have survived, but to be there.

He didn't come to see her again that night, and she assumed it must have been late when they finished dinner. Or perhaps Alexei wasn't well, or Nikolai had simply needed to be attentive to the family he so diligently worked for. She lay in bed reading one of the books he'd given her, and stayed up late to finish it. And she had just finished getting dressed when he appeared at the cottage the next morning, to inquire about his patient.

"Did you sleep well?" he asked solicitously, and she smiled and said she had, and gave him his book back, and told him how much she had enjoyed it. He seemed pleased to hear it, and had brought three more for her. "The Czarina was talking about you last night, she wants to give a small dinner party for you. Just a few friends from St. Petersburg, nothing too exhausting. Do you think you feel up to that yet?" he asked, looking worried about her. He had warned the Czarina it might still be too early, but Danina looked intrigued by the prospect.

"Maybe in a few more days. . . . What do you think, Doctor?"

"I think you're making excellent progress." He smiled at her. "I just don't want you to exhaust yourself too early. I'll take you there myself, and the moment you're tired I'll bring you back here."

"Thank you, Nikolai," she said gently. They went for a walk in the garden then. It was a cold day, and the wind was stronger than it had been the day before, and he brought her back inside in a few minutes. He was still holding her hand in his own when they returned, and neither of them seemed to notice. Her cheeks were bright pink, and her eyes bright, and she looked healthier than he had seen her since she'd been there. But she was still a long, long way from being able to go back to the ballet. She had begun exercising for half an hour a day, and had told him about it. But in his mind, he couldn't envision letting her go back to dancing with the ballet until at least April. She had to be completely well and very strong, before he would even think about it. She still had long months of recuperation ahead of her, and neither of them found it a depressing prospect. She missed the people at the ballet who were like a family to her, but in a matter of weeks she already felt completely at home here. And now the prospect of the Czarina's little dinner party greatly intrigued her.

He stayed for lunch with her that day, as he often did, and left her shortly afterward to tend to his duties at the palace, and as he so frequently did, he came back later that afternoon, and again once more after dinner. It was a routine that they both felt comfortable with, and that she now expected.

And by the next day, he had given the Czarina permission to organize the dinner for Danina. Only their closest friends would be there, and a few relatives, and of course the children. The Czar was at the front again with his troops, so he wouldn't be there.

And the following week the Grand Duchesses sent over a few dresses for her, with Demidova, their mother's maid, and two of the dresses looked splendid on Danina. She was a little slighter than they were, particularly now, after her illness, but pulling the sash of one of the gowns tighter than it was on them made her favorite of the two fit perfectly. It was a blue velvet dress, which showed her figure exceptionally well, and was trimmed in sable. It had a matching cape, and hat and muff, which would allow her to travel in the utmost warmth the short distance to the palace. And the night of the party itself, Danina

was so excited she could hardly bear it. She
had stayed in bed all that afternoon, trying
to regain her strength, and Nikolai came to
the cottage for her while she was still dress-
ing. He read one of the books of poetry he
had shared with her, while he waited, and
helped himself to a cup of steaming tea
from the silver samovar on the table. He
had become quite at home there. And at a
sound from the doorway, he glanced up,
still holding his tea, and smiled when he
saw her. She looked exquisite in her borrowed finery. And her shining dark hair was
the same color as the sable.

"You look magnificent," he said with a
look of awe. "I'm afraid you'll put everyone
else to shame, even the Grand Duchesses
and the Czarina."

"I doubt that, but you're very kind to
say so." She curtsied low, as she would have
done on the stage, but still felt how weak
her legs were as she stood again slowly.
There were no words to tell her what he felt
as he looked at her. He could not imagine
how this exquisite creature had come into
his life, so elegant, so graceful, and so
lovely. And he was as taken by her spirit as

with her beauty. He had never seen, or
known, anyone quite like her.

"Truly, you look beautiful, my dear.
Shall we go?" he asked, and she nodded, as
he helped her put the sable cape on. And
she commented again on how extraordinarily generous the Grand Duchesses had
been to send it.

They traveled the short distance to the
palace in his sled, and he covered her carefully with a heavy blanket. It was a clear,
cold night, and there were a million stars
overhead. And each of them seemed re-
flected in the candles burning brilliantly in
the windows of the palace. He took her
quickly inside, and led her upstairs to a
large, handsomely appointed salon all done
in pale silks and brocades, with marble and
malachite and treasures everywhere around
them. It was a far less formal room than
many others. And with a fire blazing in the
grate, the candlelight, and the warm recep-
tion she received, she thought she had
never felt more at home, or happier. It was
like a dream just being there with the Imperial family, and Nikolai, and their friends.
And Alexei glued himself to her all through

dinner. He sat on one side of her, at his own request, and Nikolai sat on the other, so he could "observe her condition" more closely. But there was nothing to observe except joy that night, and the delight of their friends to meet her. Everyone found her gracious, beautiful, and charming.

They spoke to her of the ballet, and were also surprised to find her knowledgeable on many subjects. Thanks to Nikolai, in recent weeks at least, she had done a great deal of reading and learning. She seemed to absorb new information like a sponge, and remember everything he told her. And listening to her now, he was oddly proud of her, as though she were his child, or something of his creating.

He allowed her to stay for quite a while, and then finally, after eleven o'clock, when he saw her growing pale, and she seemed a trifle less animated, he decided that it was wisest to withdraw her. He said something discreetly to the Czarina, and then gently told Danina that he thought it was best for her to go home now. It had been a very exciting first evening for her. And although she had loved every minute of it, she didn't argue with him. Though she hated to admit it to him, she was exhausted, and he could see it. But she was still smiling, as she leaned her head back and looked at the stars, as they rode back to the cottage.

And as he walked her inside, he stood very close to her, and put an arm around her shoulders for just a moment. She leaned her head against him, partially out of fatigue, but more out of the ease they shared, and her gratitude for all he had done for her.

"I had a wonderful time, Nikolai . . . thank you for letting me go . . . and for arranging it for me . . . everyone was so kind to me, I had a lovely time," and she mentioned one of the guests who had been very funny. "It's a shame the Czar couldn't be there." Everyone had said they missed him. She smiled then, as she looked up at her friend. "It was a lovely party."

"Everyone was in love with you tonight, Danina. Count Orlovsky thought you were particularly charming." He was well into his eighties, and had flirted with her shamelessly all evening, but even his wife thought it amusing. He had been doing precisely that and nothing more, with many beautiful women, in the sixty-five years they had been married.

"Alexei was very disappointed I wouldn't play cards with him tonight," she said as she took off her cape. It was an odd feeling, coming home together and talking about the evening, almost as though they were married. "I didn't play cards with him," she explained, "because I didn't want to be rude to the others."

"You can play cards with him another time. Perhaps tomorrow, if you're both up to it. I'm afraid he will be very tired. And you?" He looked at her then with worried eyes. "How do you feel, Danina?"

Her eyes looked vibrant and alive when she answered, their brilliant blue brighter than ever. "I feel happy and wonderful, and as though I had the most beautiful evening of my life." She stood looking at him with a small smile, as he walked slowly toward her. He still had his coat on.

"I've never known anyone like you," he said softly, as he stood directly in front of her, looking down at her, and for that one moment, he forgot entirely who she was. She was not a prima ballerina, or even his patient. She was his friend, a woman he was dazzled by, whom he had come to love, without ever expecting something like that to happen. "You are truly extraordinary," he said in a whisper, and then he took her breath away with his next words, as her eyes widened in amazement. "Danina . . . I love you. . . ." And without waiting for an answer from her, he bent gently toward her and kissed her. He held her in his arms, and she was startled to realize how powerful he was, and without thinking, she held him close to her and kissed him in answer. But within an instant, she had pulled away from him and was looking up at him in terror. What had they done? What would they do now? It would spoil everything if they did this.

"I . . . I don't . . . we can't . . . we must not, Nikolai. . . . I don't know how that happened. . . ." There were tears of distress in her eyes as he took her hands in his own. He was the first man she had ever kissed, or who had kissed her. At nineteen, he had opened a door for her that had never been opened to her before, and she had no idea what to do now.

"I know exactly how it happened, Danina," he said, sounding calmer than he felt. As he looked at her, his heart was pounding. And now he was terrified to lose her. Perhaps with one brave gesture he had driven her away from him forever, and the prospect of that filled him with terror. Whatever happened now, he could not lose her. "I fell in love with you the first time I saw you. I never thought you would live through the night. But I was haunted by you for all those days, you were an illusion of grace and beauty, an injured butterfly I thought would not be spared. But I had no idea who you were, I knew nothing of you . . . until now . . . until you came here, and we have sat talking every day. And now I love everything about you, your mind, your spirit, your kind heart. . . . Danina, I cannot live without you." It was a plea for clemency as well as a gift he gave her, and she knew it.

"But Nikolai, you are married," she said, with tears in her eyes, and a look of sorrow. "We cannot do this. We must not . . . we must forget it. . . ."

"I am not married, except in name. You know that, even from the little I have told you. Surely, you must have sensed it. I have never done anything like this before. . . . I swear it . . . you are the first woman I have ever loved. I'm not sure Marie and I ever loved each other. Not like this. And certainly not now. Danina, I swear to you . . . she hates me."

"Perhaps you're wrong, perhaps you do not truly understand her feelings, or her unhappiness being here in Russia. Perhaps you should move to England with her." She was pacing now, and looking agitated and distraught, and he was more than ever afraid to lose her. And then she turned to him, and said the words he feared the most, other than if she had said she didn't love him. But the moment she kissed him, he knew she did. She felt the same way that he did, although she was deathly afraid to admit it. "I must go back to St. Petersburg. You must let me. I cannot stay here."

"You can't go back. You're not strong

enough to live in that freezing barracks, or to dance again. You will not be well enough for months, you'll fall ill again. It could be disastrous for you." He was near tears as he said it. "I beg you, don't leave here." He couldn't bear the thought of her being far away now.

"I cannot be near you . . . we will both know now that we carry in our hearts a terrible secret, a dreadful sin, for which we will be punished."

"I have already lived my punishment for fifteen years. You cannot condemn me to that life forever."

"What are you saying to me?" Her eyes leapt and she covered her mouth with her hands, as though in horror at what he was proposing.

"I am saying I will do anything for you. I will leave my wife, my family. . . . Danina, I will do anything to be with you."

"You *must not* do that, or even say it. I can't bear thinking of your doing something so terrible. . . . Nikolai, think of your children!" She was in tears as she said it, but so was he when he answered.

"I have thought of them a thousand

times, every day, ever since I met you. But they are not babies anymore. They are twelve and fourteen, in a few years they will be grown men, and I cannot live with a woman I cannot bear for the rest of my life in their honor . . . nor forsake the only woman I have ever loved. Danina, don't run away, please . . . stay here with me . . . we will talk about it. . . . I will not do anything you don't want me to do. I promise."

"Then you must not speak of this again. *Ever.* We must both forget you ever said it, if we can. I cannot be anything more to you than I am. Your life is here, with the Czar, and your family. Mine is at the ballet. I cannot give myself to you, I have no life to give you. My life belongs to the ballet, until I am too old to dance, and then I will give it to the children, like Madame Markova."

"Are you telling me you must be a nun to be a dancer?" It was the first he had heard of it, although he knew she had never been in love, or been close to men, because she had said so in one of their many conversations.

"Madame Markova says that an impure life, a life of men, is distracting. One cannot be a great dancer if one wants to be a harlot." She said it bluntly and he looked startled.

"I was hardly suggesting you be a harlot, Danina. I was telling you I love you, and want to marry you, if Marie will divorce me."

"And I'm telling you I can't do it. I belong at the ballet. It is my life, it is all I know, it is what I was born to. And I will not let you destroy your life for me."

"You were born to love, and be loved, as we all were, and to be surrounded by a husband and children who love you, not to dance in drafty halls, breaking your back and risking your health until you die, or are too old and crippled to serve any longer. You deserve more than that, and I want to give it to you."

"But you cannot," she said, sounding distressed again. "You don't have it to give. And what if Marie would not agree to divorce you?"

"She would be happy to go back to England. She would gladly pay for her freedom by agreeing to divorce me."

"And the scandal? The Czar could no

longer have you near his family, nor should
he. You would be an outcast, a disgrace. I
will not let you do that. You must forget
me." The tears ran down her face as she
said it.

"I will forget everything we said tonight," he said with difficulty, "if you promise you will stay here. I will never mention it
again. You have my solemn promise." A
promise it nearly killed him to offer.

"All right." She sighed deeply and
turned her back to him, her head bowed, as
he watched her, aching to put his arms
around her, but he knew he couldn't. She
looked desperately unhappy, but not nearly
as unhappy as he was. "I'll think about staying," was all she said, and she did not turn
around again to look at him. She couldn't.
She was still crying. "You must go now." He
could not see her face as she said it, only
the straight young back, and the proud tilt
of her head, and the shining dark hair cas-
cading past her shoulders. And he longed to
touch it, and hold her.

"Good night, Danina," he said in a
voice filled with regret and longing, and
then a moment later she heard the door

close behind him, and she turned to look at it, sobbing.

She could not believe what they had done, what he had said, and the worst of it was that she also knew she loved him. But he was a married man, and she could not let him destroy his life, or lose his work or his children, for her sake. She loved him too much to let him do that. And she had her obligations to the ballet. She remembered all too clearly a lifetime of Madame Markova's dire warnings. Madame Markova had always told her she was different, that she didn't need a man, that she must remain pure, that she had to live for and grow through her art, her dancing had to come before anything else in her life, and it had till now. But now suddenly with Nikolai, she saw that it could be so different. A life with him would mean an eternity of happiness, but not if it cost him everything he held dear to have her. She couldn't let him do that.

She knew she should go back to St. Petersburg, but she couldn't bear leaving him now. She couldn't think of not seeing him every day, any more than he could give up seeing her. All they had to do now was pretend this had never happened between them, which would be far from easy. But she was determined to do it. And as she walked into her room, and began to undress, she felt her knees begin to shake violently. She had to sit down, and as she did, all she could think of were his lips on hers, and what she had felt when he had kissed her. But no matter what she felt for him now, she knew with her entire heart and soul that she could never have him. But at least, if she stayed, they could still see each other. She sat looking at her reflection in the mirror, thinking of him, and wondering how they could do it. It was going to be anything but easy.

# Chapter 4

Nikolai didn't come to see her at all for the next two days, nor did he go to the palace. But finally he sent her two new books with a message that he had caught a bad cold and didn't want to give it to her. And he would see her as soon as he was no longer contagious. She had no idea if it was true or not, but if so, if nothing else, his absence was at least convenient. And it gave them both time to regain control of themselves, and try to forget what had happened.

But without his visits, she paced uncomfortably around her small house, tried to sleep and found she couldn't, and by the end of the first day had a dreadful headache, and refused to take anything for it.

Her nurses found her uncharacteristically short-tempered and fretful, and she apologized to them a thousand times for her ill humor, and blamed it on her migraine. And by the end of the second day, she was despondent. She wondered if he was angry at her, if he regretted what he had said and done, if he had been drunk and she didn't know it, if she would never see him again. She could bear burying their secret and never mentioning it again, but what she realized now with full force, was that she couldn't bear not seeing him.

And when he appeared at last, as she stood in her small living room, watching the snow fall in her garden, she didn't hear him come in. She turned, with tears rolling down her cheeks, thinking of him, and when she saw him, without thinking, she flew across the room into his arms, and told him how much she had missed him. He was not sure what it meant at first, if she had changed her mind and was willing to go forward with him, or simply what she said, that she had missed him.

"I've missed you too," he said in a voice that still sounded hoarse, so she knew that his excuse for not seeing her had been sincere, and that relieved her. "Very much," he said, smiling at her. But this time, he was not foolish enough to kiss her. He had taken her at her word two days before, and was determined not to cross that line again, unless she invited him to do so. And she herself made no move to kiss him. She went straight to the samovar, and poured him a cup of tea, and handed it to him. And as she did so, her hand was shaking but she was beaming.

"I'm so glad you've been ill . . . oh . . . I mean . . . that sounds terrible. . . ." She laughed for the first time in two days, and he laughed too as he sat down near her in the cottage's small, cozy parlor. "I was afraid you didn't want to see me."

"You know that's not true," he said with eyes that told her everything she longed to hear but would never allow him to say again. She was desperately happy to see him. "I didn't want to make you ill after all you've been through. But I'm feeling much better."

"I'm glad to hear it," she said, feeling a

trifle awkward with him, but looking at him intensely. He looked even more handsome to her now, taller and more powerful. In an odd way he was hers now, and she knew it, and it made him even more precious to her, even if they could never have what they both longed for. And with good reason. "Were you very sick?" she asked solicitously, and he was touched. She looked incredibly pretty in a pink wool dress that made her seem even younger than he remembered. She had looked very glamorous and very grown up in the blue velvet gown two nights before, and now she looked like a young girl, which more than ever made him want to kiss her. But this time, he knew he couldn't.

"I was not as sick as you were. Thank God. I'm fine now."

"You shouldn't be out in the snow," she chided him, and he smiled at her in answer.

"I wanted to come and see Alexei," he explained, but his eyes told her something else as well. He had wanted to see her even more than Alexei.

"Will you stay for lunch?" she asked

politely, and he nodded and smiled with pleasure.

"I'd like that." And as he said it, they both thought that they could do this. They could spend time together, just as they had before, without ever divulging their secret, even to each other. But she had already begun to wonder what would happen when she went back to St. Petersburg in a month or two. Would they forget each other, or would he come to see her? Would it just become a cherished memory, and their love for each other fade like the residue of her influenza? It was already hard to imagine leaving.

They talked well into the afternoon, she returned some of his books to him, and he promised to come and see her again on his way home that evening, and everything seemed normal again when he left her. But he did not return that evening after all, and instead sent her a message. Alexei wasn't well, and Nikolai was spending the night at the palace with his patient and Dr. Botkin. Because of his hemophilia, the child needed careful observation, and Nikolai didn't think it wise to leave him. But Danina understood, and curled up in her bed with one of his books, feeling relieved to have seen him that morning. His two-day absence after their drama after the dinner party had been excruciating for her. Her migraine had disappeared the moment she saw him.

And it was a relief to her again when he appeared the next morning to have breakfast with her. But even she was not unaware that there was suddenly a greater intensity between them. Although they had agreed not to discuss their feelings for each other again, it was suddenly clear that his visits meant the world to her, and he himself had begun to feel anxious whenever he wasn't with her. But they were both still convinced that they could control the blaze of what they felt, forever if they had to, and she was determined to keep it in check, and never speak of it again for their entire lifetimes. Nikolai was growing less certain day by day that he could do it, but knew he had to do as she wished, for fear that if he didn't, he would lose her.

He spoke at length of Alexei that day, and explained the nature of his illness in detail to her. And it led them into a discussion about the joys of having children. He told her that she must not deprive herself of that, that he felt certain she would make a wonderful mother. But she only shook her head, and reminded him of her commitment to the ballet. And he told her again that he thought her unnecessary zeal on that subject unreasonable and unhealthy.

"Madame Markova would never forgive me if I left," she said quietly. "She has given her entire life to us, and always will," she said simply to him after breakfast. "She expects the same of me."

"Why you more than any of the others?" he asked pointedly, and this time she laughed when she answered, and for the first time in days, her eyes seemed full of mischief.

"Because I'm a better dancer than they are."

He smiled broadly as she said it. "And certainly more modest," he teased. "But you're right. You are a better dancer, but that's still not a reason to give your life up for it."

"Ballet is more than just dancing,

Nikolai. It is a way of life, a spirit, a part of your soul, a religion."

"You're crazy, Danina Petroskova, but I love you." The words had just slipped out, and he glanced up at her in terror, but she said nothing. She knew it had been a mistake, an accident, and she decided to ignore it.

It had stopped snowing again by then, after nearly two days of heavy snowfall, and they walked out into her garden, and a moment later, she began pelting him with snowballs. He loved being with her so much more than he could tell her, he loved her childlike spirit, coupled with her great intensity, and devotion to all that she believed in. She was an extraordinary young woman. And by the time he left her that afternoon, to go home and change after his night with his young charge, they were feeling relaxed and at ease with each other again. The cloud that had hung over them for the past few days seemed to have dispelled to a tolerable degree, and they were both confident that they could live with the restrictions Danina had imposed on them. And at the end of another week, they were completely comfortable again with their arrangement.

Nikolai came to see her at least twice a day, and whenever possible, even more often. He frequently had lunch or dinner with her, and sometimes arrived early enough to spend breakfast with her. The weather had been severe that month, and they stayed inside most of the time, but by the end of January it was slowly getting better. As was her health. She was making steady progress in her recovery, but she was still a long way from returning to the ballet, and Danina didn't push it. She had originally begged Madame Markova to only stay a month, but it had always been Nikolai's recommendation that she stay until March or April. And when she wrote to Madame Markova again, she told her that she had agreed to it. It was exactly what she needed. And Madame Markova was relieved to hear it. As was the Czarina. They loved having her with them.

The Grand Duchesses came to tea whenever they could and weren't busy with their nursing or their lessons. And Alexei loved playing cards with her. She seemed a perfect addition to the family, as far as he was concerned. And it was Alexei who announced that she had to come to his parents' ball on the first of February, it was the first one they had given in ages. The Czarina had been feeling so sorry for her daughters having had no fun in so long, and no break in their nursing, that she had convinced her husband that a ball would lift everyone's spirits. And after telling Danina about it, he informed his mother that he wanted her invited.

The Czarina said there wasn't anything she'd like better, and without waiting for an answer from Danina, she sent a number of gowns over for her to try, just as she had for their far less formal dinner. But the gowns she sent this time were truly spectacular, and Danina was overwhelmed when she saw them.

There were satins and silks, and velvets and brocades, they were fit for a queen, or for a Czarina, and Danina was almost embarrassed to wear them. She chose a white satin finally, with a gold brocade bustier, which cinched her tiny waist in so tightly that she looked like a fairy queen more than just a ballerina. She looked, as Alexei said, when she tried it on for him, like a fairy princess. Nikolai had not yet seen it, but had heard all about it. And the white satin cape which went with it was lined in the same gold brocade as the bustier, and trimmed in ermine. It was indeed very regal, and with Danina's dark hair she looked more striking than ever. In some ways, it felt like a costume to her, but it was more beautiful than any she had seen or worn, or even dreamed of. And Nikolai was pleased to hear that she was going. As he had before, he cautioned her not to exhaust herself, and to leave as soon as she was tired. But he had no objection to her attending the Czar's ball, and offered to take her there himself, as he had to their dinner.

The ball itself was an unusual event these days. The Imperial family had canceled all formal social occasions due to the war, with the exception of this one. And there was no way of knowing when they would give another. The Czar was coming home from the front for it, and everyone was happy he was going to be there.

"Won't your wife come at least to this

one?" Danina asked Nikolai cautiously when they spoke of it the day before the ball, but he shook his head and looked annoyed. At one time he would have told Marie how rude it was of her to refuse their invitation, but this time he really didn't mind, for reasons that were obvious to Danina. She had already told herself that she would dance with him once or twice, if he asked her, but it would mean nothing. The revelation that had been made to her two weeks before seemed to have receded into the mists since then. They were once again just friends, and nothing more alarming.

"Of course not," was all Nikolai said in answer to her question. "She detests balls . . . or anything that does not involve horses." And then he changed the subject, and he smiled when he said that Alexei had said she looked "pretty good" in the dress his mother had lent her. But "pretty good" did not in any way prepare Nikolai for the way Danina looked when she emerged from her bedroom in the white satin and gold brocade gown trimmed in ermine. She looked like a young queen, with her hair piled on her head in a little crown of loose curls, and the pearl earrings that were the only thing she had of her mother's. She was glad she had thought to bring them with her.

She took Nikolai's breath away, as he looked at her, and for a long moment he said nothing. There were tears in his eyes, and he only prayed she would not see them.

"Do I look all right?" she asked nervously, as she would have to one of her brothers.

"I don't even know what to tell you. I have never seen anyone look as beautiful as you do."

"You're silly," she smiled shyly at him, "but thank you. It's a lovely dress, isn't it?"

"On you, it is." Her waist was the size of a small child's, her bosom revealed just enough, without being vulgar or offensive. Nothing about her could have offended, and in his tails, he seemed the perfect escort for her as he led her off to the party at the Catherine Palace. The Catherine Palace was on the grounds of Tsarskoe Selo as well. It was far grander and more ornate than the Alexander Palace, where they lived. And the Czarina preferred to use it only for state occasions, although at the moment, part of it was being used to nurse the wounded soldiers. The palace had been redone by Catherine the Great, and was originally designed by Rostrelli, and the brilliant gold roof made it look extremely formal and opulent as they approached it.

But even among all the glittering gowns and jewels and visiting royalty, Danina caused a noticeable sensation. Everyone wanted to know who she was, where she was from, and where she had been hiding. And several dashing young noblemen were convinced she was a princess. Her regal bearing and the graceful way she moved caught everyone's attention. And as soon as she saw her, Danina was quick to thank the Czarina discreetly for the dress she was wearing.

"You must keep the gown, my dear. None of us will ever be able to wear it as you do." And Danina could see instantly that she meant it, and was even more touched by her continuing generosity and kindness.

The dinner for four hundred guests was

in the Silver Room. The gentlemen withdrew for a short while after that to the famous Amber Room, and then the entire party moved into the Great Gallery for dancing. It was an exquisite evening. And Danina had more energy than she'd had since she'd been ill. She was excited just to be there. It was a night she wanted to remember, in every impeccable detail, forever.

And when Nikolai led her onto the dance floor, she felt her heart give a little flutter, but not for an instant did she allow herself to think of what he had said to her two weeks before. That chapter in their lives was already over. All they had between them now, or so she told herself, was camaraderie and friendship. But the look in his eyes as he swept her around the floor gracefully in a waltz told an entirely different story. He looked unbearably proud of her, and his gentle touch as he held her as close as he dared would have told her all he couldn't say, if she had let it. Even the Czar mentioned something to his wife when they were dancing.

"I'm afraid Nikolai is smitten with our

young visitor from the ballet," he said by way of observation, without criticism or comment.

"I don't think so, my dear." The Czarina denied it. She had seen them together frequently, and saw nothing unseemly in their friendship, or behavior.

"It's a shame he's married to that dreadful Englishwoman," he said, and the Czarina smiled in answer. She wasn't fond of her either.

"I think he's only concerned with Danina's health," she said firmly, far more naive than her husband.

"She looks lovely in that dress she's wearing. Is it one of yours?" The Czarina was wearing a red velvet gown that was spectacular, with a full set of his mother's rubies, which became her remarkably. She was a beautiful woman, and he loved her dearly. They were both happy he was home again, and at least able to forget the war for a few brief moments.

"It's Olga's actually, but it looks so pretty on Danina, I told her to keep it."

"She has a lovely figure." He smiled down at his wife then, no longer interested in talking about their guest. "But so do you, my love. I think Mama's rubies look extremely well on you."

"Thank you," she said with a smile, and eventually they left the floor and circulated among their guests. It was a most successful party. And Nikolai and Danina danced half the night away. It was hard to believe she'd ever been ill, and she certainly didn't feel it as she danced with him. It was after midnight when he finally urged her to sit down for a while and rest, before she wore herself out completely. She was having such a good time, she didn't want to stop dancing for a minute.

He brought her a glass of champagne, and smiled as he handed it to her. Her cheeks were flushed, her eyes bluer than ever, and her bosom tantalizing and creamy. He had to force himself to look away for a moment. But when he looked at her again, he found he couldn't resist her, and moments later, he was dancing with her again, and she looked happier and lovelier than ever.

"I feel like a dismal failure as the guardian of your health," he confessed as they danced another waltz, looking as though they had danced together forever. The only time he had ever danced with his wife was at their wedding. "I should be forcing you to go home and rest, but I can't bring myself to do it. I'm afraid you're going to be exhausted to the point of feeling ill tomorrow."

"It will have been worth it," she said, laughing up at him with the sound that enchanted him unbearably. Just as she did, he wanted the night to go on forever.

It was after three when they finally left, and they were among the last to leave, after Danina had thanked the Czar and Czarina profusely. It had been an unforgettable evening, and they thanked her warmly for coming and, like Nikolai, voiced the hope that she hadn't done herself any damage by dancing so much and staying so long, when perhaps she should have been resting.

"I will stay in bed all day tomorrow," she promised, and the Czarina urged her to do it. It would be a shame if she fell ill again because of the party.

But she was still in high spirits as they went back to her cottage. It was a lovely night, with a sky filled with stars, fresh snow on the ground, and all she could remember now was the endless dancing. Several people had asked her to dance, and she had danced with them willingly, but most of the evening she had spent in Nikolai's arms, and had to admit she preferred it. She was still chatting happily about all of it as they walked into her cottage, and he helped her take the ermine cape off. And just as he had all night, he couldn't help staring at her, and how beautiful she was in all her finery. More so than any other woman he'd seen all evening.

"Would you like something to drink?" she asked him easily, she was too excited to sleep, and she hated to have it end now. And he had much the same feeling, as he poured himself a glass of brandy, and they went to sit in front of the fire the maids had left for them, and to talk about the evening. She surprised him by sitting at his feet in the splendid gown, and leaning her head against him. She was thinking about the evening, and was smiling into the fire dreamily, as he gently stroked her hair, and felt the sheer pleasure of having her lean against him.

"I will never forget this night," she said quietly, happy to just be there with him, not wanting anything more than she could have from him.

"Nor will I," he said, touching her long graceful arm with his hand, and then resting it on her shoulder. She felt so delicate and looked so fragile, and as she turned to look up at him she was smiling. "I'm so happy when I'm with you, Danina," he confessed, afraid to go too far again, and offend her. But it was so hard not to tell her how he felt about her.

"So am I, Nikolai. We have been very lucky to find each other," she said, and meant it, not intending to tease him, but merely to celebrate their friendship. But she was making it more difficult for him than ever.

"You make me dream again," he said sadly, holding his brandy, "of things I gave up years ago." At thirty-nine, he felt as though he had a lifetime behind him. A lifetime of lost hopes, and shattered illusions and disappointment. And now, in her, he saw the dream again, and yet he couldn't have it with her. "I love being with you." And then, feeling too far away from her, he slipped onto the floor next to her, and they sat side by side looking into the fire, at their dreams, as he put an arm around her. "I never want to hurt you, Danina," he said gently. "I want you to always be happy."

"I am happy here," she said honestly, and she had been happy at the ballet. She had never really known unhappiness, only endless discipline and great devotion to what she'd been doing. Hers was a life of passion. And then she turned to look at him, and saw that there were tears in his eyes, as there had been earlier when he first saw her that night, but this time she saw them clearly, the first time she hadn't been as certain. "Are you sad, Nikolai?" She felt sorry for him. She knew his life wasn't easy for him. Although she chose not to acknowledge it, she knew how desperately unhappy he was at home, with a woman who didn't love him.

"A little bit perhaps . . . but mostly very happy to be here with you."

"You deserve more than that," she said quietly, realizing that he asked very little of her, and gave of his heart completely. She felt unfair to him suddenly. She had silenced him for her own purposes, so she would not be uncomfortable, but she had forced him to deny his feelings. "You deserve great happiness for all the kind things you do. You give so much to so many . . . and to me," she added softly.

"It's easy to give to you. I only wish I had more to give you. Life is cruel sometimes, isn't it? You find precisely what you want . . . too late to have it."

"Perhaps it isn't," she said in a whisper, feeling drawn to him as she had never been to any man, except him, when he had kissed her. He didn't dare ask her what she meant, but only looked at her, and her eyes were beckoning him with an openness and love for him that was so evident, he could not mistake their invitation.

"I don't want to hurt you . . . or upset you. . . . I love you too much to do that," he said, trying to hold back all that he felt for her, for her sake.

"I love you, Nikolai," she said simply,

and without hesitating this time, or fearing anything, he took her gently in his arms and kissed her, and it was all that they had each dreamed of. They were ready for it this time, it did not take them by surprise, or frighten them, and this time it was what they both wanted.

They kissed for a long time in front of the fire, and he held her in his arms, until the fire began to dim and she began to shiver, with the chill and their excitement. She knew that she was his now.

"Come . . . you will catch a cold, my love. I'll put you to bed, and go," he whispered in the last glow of the fire, and then he led her to her bedroom. "Shall I help you out of the dress?" It looked complicated and she couldn't manage it alone, and with a small smile she nodded. She would have had to sleep in it without one of the maids to help her undo it.

She looked like a child as he gently lifted the dress away from her, standing there with her lithe, thin, youthful dancer's body, and her eyes were huge as she looked at him with something innocent and longing. "It's too late for you to go home," she whispered cautiously, not sure what to say to him, or how to begin it. She had never done this before, and couldn't imagine it now. But she also could no longer imagine not being with him.

"What are you saying to me?" he whispered back in the chill of the early morning, looking worried.

"Stay with me. We don't have to do anything we don't want to. I just want you here with me." He belonged there, and she knew it, just as he did.

"Oh, Danina," he said softly, knowing that it was the beginning of a new life, and the end of an old one. For both of them, it was a moment filled with promise and decision. "I want so much to be here with you." It was all he had wanted since the moment he met her, even more so since she had come here. And he realized now this was why he had done everything he could to bring her to this cottage, to be near him.

They undressed carefully, and a moment later were in her huge comfortable bed, snuggled deep under the covers, and as she glanced up at him in the darkness, she giggled, and sounded like a schoolgirl.

"Why are you laughing, silly girl?" he asked, still whispering, as though someone could hear them. But there was no one there at that hour. They were entirely alone, with their secrets and their love for each other.

"It just seems funny. . . . I was so afraid of what I felt for you . . . and of what I knew of your feelings, and now here we are, like two naughty children."

"Not naughty children, my love . . . happy ones . . . maybe we have a right to this after all . . . perhaps it was meant to be. My destiny, and yours. Danina, I have never loved any woman as I love you." And with that, he kissed her quietly and firmly, and her passion rose with his, as he taught her all she had never known and never dreamed of, and never thought of finding with him. But it was all there, waiting for her, the gifts, the grace, the love they had each longed for. And as she slept in his arms at last, he held her close and smiled at the generosity of the gods for giving her to him.

"Good night, my love," he whispered gratefully, and fell fast asleep beside her.

# Chapter 5

*T*he secret they shared grew between them like a field of wild-
flowers in summer. He came to see her
every day, as he had before, but now he
stayed much longer, while still managing to
perform his duties at the palace. And at
night, when he had completed what he had
to do there, he returned to her, and slept
with her. He had told his wife that they
needed him at night now to stay with
Alexei. And she seemed to have no interest,
and no objection.

Danina was thrilled to have him. He
taught her things that bound her to him,
and they gave their hearts and souls to each
other. They told each other everything, and
had no secrets from each other. Their

hopes, their dreams, their childhood fears, and the only real terror they shared was that they might one day lose each other. They had not yet sorted out what would happen when she left there. Because they both knew that eventually she'd have to. And after that, they would have to do something about their future. But he had said nothing to his wife yet.

They just wanted to enjoy what they had, for now, before they caused any major explosions. And once their happiness became real to them, February flew past them like an express train, and March along with it. She had been there for three months, when she finally began talking, with regret, of returning to the ballet. She couldn't begin to imagine how she would do it. And even Madame Markova had been asking her pointedly about when she planned to return for classes and training. It was going to take her months to get back what she had lost in her months of illness. Compared to her grueling daily routine at the ballet, the modest exercises she'd done here meant nothing. Even with her daily exercise, it was no way near enough for the ballet. And finally, with regret, she promised to return to St. Petersburg at the end of April. But the thought of leaving Nikolai was almost more than she could bear now.

They spoke of it seriously late one afternoon, three weeks before she was scheduled to leave him. He thought it was time for him to speak to Marie, and suggest that she return to England, with the children. The deception had to end now. But he was not yet sure what Danina wanted to do about the ballet. She had her own choices to make on that subject.

"What do you think Marie will say when you tell her?"

"I think she'll be relieved," he said honestly. He was sure of that, but not as sure that she would agree to divorce him. He preferred not to tell her about Danina if he could help it. There were more than enough reasons to end it with his wife, without complicating matters further.

"And the boys? Will she let you see them?" She looked worried, this was all she had tormented herself about before they began their affair, and why she had hesitated to do so. But they could never have stopped themselves. That had been a fantasy. She knew that clearly now. This was real, and they would never have been able to deny it.

"I don't know what she'll do about the boys," he said honestly. "I may have to wait to see them until they're older." The pain of it showed in his eyes, and Danina saw it with anguish for him. "And Madame Markova?" he asked her in return. That was almost as big a question, though somewhat simpler in his eyes, but not Danina's.

"I will talk to her when I go back to St. Petersburg," she said, trying to still the fear she felt, or the sense that she was about to betray her. Madame Markova expected so much from her, had given so much to her, and she would be devastated if Danina left the ballet. But for her, everything had changed now. Her life belonged to Nikolai, and she could no longer ignore that.

Miraculously, what they had shared seemed to have gone unnoticed by everyone but the maids in her cottage, and remarkably they had been discreet about it thus far. No one in the Imperial family had ever commented on it to Nikolai, and even

Alexei, who spent a great deal of time with them, had no sense that things had changed between them.

But in the last three weeks they shared, there was a kind of desperation to what they were both feeling. Such as it had been, as idyllic and perfect as the time was, it was about to end now. A new life was about to be entered into. And Danina was worried about it. If she left the ballet to be with him, where would she live, and who would support her? If he divorced Marie, would the scandal cost him his sacred place in the Imperial family? It was a great deal for them to consider and think of. But he had already promised that he would find her a place to live, and support her, though she didn't want to be a burden to him, and thought she should stay with the ballet until Marie left for England.

In the end, he decided to tell Marie after Danina left, so as to shield her from any reaction to the scandal it might cause at home or in the palace. And to both of them, it seemed the wisest decision. He would come to see her at the ballet as soon as he could, and tell her what had happened, and then they could make their plans from that moment onward. Besides, the ballet needed time to replace her. Although she had been ill for months, they were still counting on her for performances that summer and the following winter. It was possible, she had explained to him, that she might even have to wait until the end of the year to leave them, but he said he understood that. They would spend as much time together as they could, in spite of the demands on both of them, and the heavy training she would have to undertake now. But she was ready and strong again, and happier than she had ever been, with her love for him, and all that they had promised to each other.

But despite all the promises, their last week was an agony of sorrow. They spent every moment together that they could, and for the first time, the Czarina noticed how close they were, and agreed with what her husband had noticed earlier. She was almost certain Nikolai and Danina were in love with each other. The Czar was on leave again at the time, and she mentioned it to him.

"I don't blame him," he said quietly to his wife late one night, as Nikolai and Danina were spending one of their last nights in the cottage. "She's very lovely."

"Do you think he'll leave his wife for her?" The Czarina was beginning to wonder, and the Czar said he couldn't guess at other people's madness. "And if he does, will you mind?" she asked him, and the head of the Imperial family pondered the question, uncertain of his decision on the subject.

"It will depend how he does it. If it's done quietly, it shouldn't affect anything. If it becomes a terrible scandal that upsets everyone, we'll have to think about it." It was a sensible conclusion, and the Czarina was relieved to hear it. She didn't want to lose Nikolai as Alexei's doctor. But she also wondered if Danina would leave the ballet. She was very young, had a lot invested in it, and she was their most famous prima. To the Czarina it seemed a little like leaving the convent, not easily done, and she was sure the ballet would do everything they could to keep her. It was going to be a difficult decision, if Danina chose to do it, and she felt sorry for her. She hoped things went well for both of them, if they decided to embark on a new life together. In the months that Danina had been there, they had all come to love her.

They gave a small dinner for her the night before she left, with the children and a few close friends present, both physicians, and a handful of people who had met and fallen in love with Danina, and she had tears in her eyes when she thanked them, and promised to return. The Czarina asked her to come and visit them at Livadia that summer, as she had done the year before with Madame Markova, and they promised to come and watch her perform as soon as she was dancing.

"I'll really teach you to swim this time," Alexei promised and gave her a gift that she knew he hated to part with. It was a small jade Fabergé frog that he loved because he thought it was so ugly. But he gave it to her, awkwardly wrapped in a drawing he had made her. The girls had each written her poems, and made lovely watercolors for her, and together they gave her a photograph of all of them, with Danina. She was

still deeply touched when she and Nikolai
went back to the cottage for their last night
together.

"I can't bear to leave you tomorrow,"
she said sadly, after they made love, and lay
in each other's arms, talking until morning.
She couldn't believe her stay here was over,
even if they told each other a new life was
beginning. That night when they came
home from dinner, he had given her a gold
locket on a chain, with a photograph of him
in it. He looked so much like the Czar in
the photograph that she wasn't even sure it
was Nikolai at first, but it was, and she
promised to wear it every moment when
she wasn't dancing.

The last hours they shared were an agony for both of them, and they both cried
when he put her on the train for the short
trip she had to make to return to the ballet
in St. Petersburg. She didn't want him to go
back with her, for fear that Madame Markova would instantly see what had happened between them. She believed that her
mentor had mystical powers and was all-
seeing and all-knowing, but he had agreed
not to go with her. He was going to speak to

Marie that afternoon, and promised to let Danina know immediately what had happened.

But as he stood on the platform, watching the train, they both felt their hearts breaking, and a chapter ending that they had cherished. She hung out the window for as long as she could, and saw him standing there, waving at her, his eyes locked in hers, her locket around her neck, as she felt it with trembling fingers. He had shouted to her that he loved her, as they pulled away, and had kissed her so many times in the cottage before they left that her lips were sore, and she had had to comb her hair again twice before she left him. They were like two children being torn from their parents, and it reminded her more than a little of when her father had taken her to the ballet to live. She was just as terrified now, possibly even more so.

Madame Markova was waiting for her in the station when she arrived in St. Petersburg. She seemed taller, and thinner, and looked more severe than ever. Danina thought she looked suddenly older, and she felt as though she had been gone forever.

But Madame Markova kissed her warmly, and looked deeply pleased when she saw her. Despite what had happened to Danina while she was away, she had missed Madame Markova immensely.

"You look well, Danina. Happy and rested."

"Thank you, Madame. Everyone was wonderful to me."

"So I understood from your letters." There was an edge to her voice, a toughness Danina had forgotten in her. It was what drove everyone well beyond their capabilities, to please her. But she was cool as they drove to the ballet in a taxi. And Danina tried to fill the void, by telling her about her adventures with the Imperial family, and the parties she'd been to. But she had the very clear sense that she had somehow displeased her mistress, and more than ever it made Danina long for the life she had left behind at Tsarskoe Selo. But she knew she had to return now to her obligations.

"When do I begin classes again?" Danina asked as she watched the familiar city roll past them.

"Tomorrow morning. I suggest you

commence exercising this afternoon to prepare yourself. I assume you have done nothing to maintain yourself during your convalescence?" Aside from Danina's few daily exercises, she had assumed correctly, and did not look pleased about it when Danina nodded.

"The doctor didn't think it wise, Madame," was her only excuse. She did not even bother to mention the half hour of exercise she had done daily. She knew that to her ballet mistress, it would seem a negligible effort.

Madame Markova stared ahead in silence and said nothing, as the atmosphere grew thick between them.

She had been reassigned to her old room, and it filled Danina's heart with sadness when she saw the old building. Instead of feeling like a homecoming to her, it was only a reminder of how far she was now from Nikolai and their nights in the beloved cottage. She couldn't imagine spending a night without him, but she was going to have to. They both had long roads to travel separately until they could once again be together, hopefully forever.

She had thought of saying something to Madame Markova immediately about her plans, but she had decided to wait until she heard from Nikolai about the divorce and Marie's move to England. It all depended on how fast things were moving. And beneath the thin surface of her blouse, she felt the comfort of her locket.

Everyone was warming up, or rehearsing, or exercising, or in class when she arrived, and there was no one in the stark room she had left four months before. It looked strange to her now, and pitifully ugly as she changed into a leotard and ballet shoes, and hurried down the stairs to the studio she normally warmed up in. And when she got there, she saw Madame Markova, sitting quietly in a corner, watching the others. Her presence made Danina feel slightly uncomfortable, but she got to work at the barre, and was stunned to discover how stiff she was, how awkward her movements, how unwilling her limbs were to do what they had been trained for.

"You have a lot of work to do, Danina," Madame Markova said sternly, as Danina nodded. Her body had become her enemy in four brief months, and did none of the things she expected of it. And that night, when she went to bed, every muscle she had used for the first time in months was screaming at her. She could hardly sleep for the pain she felt everywhere, nor get up the next day, as she felt every muscle in her body tighten. The effect of the past four months of indolence and happiness had been brutal.

But no less so than the rigorous training she launched into at five o'clock that morning. She was in her first class at six, and worked until nine o'clock that night, and through most of it, Madame Markova watched her.

"Your gift was not given to waste," she said harshly after the first class, and then warned her even more sharply that she would never get back what she had lost if she didn't push herself well beyond her limits. And then she added, "If you are not willing to pay for it with blood, Danina, you do not deserve it." She was visibly furious at what Danina had lost in her months away from the ballet, and she reminded her unkindly that night that her place as their first prima was not simply something they owed her, but an honor she had to earn back if she intended to regain her position.

Danina was in tears when she went to bed that night, and again several times the following day, and finally at the end of the second day, exhausted beyond anything she had ever known, she sat down and wrote Nikolai a letter, telling him what she was going through and how much she missed him. More than she had ever thought possible when she left him.

The torture they put her through went on for days, and by the end of the first week, Danina was sorry she had ever returned to the ballet, particularly if she was leaving. What was the point, and what did she have to prove to them now, if she was going to return to Nikolai and stop dancing? But she felt she owed it to them to finish honorably, and even if it killed her, she was determined to do so. But at that point, dying from sheer exhaustion and endless pain seemed not only desirable, but likely.

It was at the end of the second week that Madame Markova called her into her office, and Danina wondered what it meant. In the past thirteen years, she had rarely been there, though others had been, and always emerged in tears, sometimes to leave the ballet within hours. Danina couldn't help wondering if this was to be her fate now. Madame Markova sat very still across the desk from her, and stared hard at her protégée before speaking.

"I can see what has happened to you, from the way you dance, from the way you are working. You don't need to tell me anything, Danina, if you do not choose to." Danina had been planning to tell her everything, but not like this, not yet, not until she heard from Nikolai, and so far she hadn't, and she was worried about it. And at times, Madame Markova was right, her love for Nikolai was distracting her from dancing. She couldn't completely give her all to her dancing, as she once had. It was more something spiritual than something physical that had happened. But it amazed her that Madame Markova could see it.

"I'm not sure what you mean, Madame. I have been working very hard since I got back." There were tears in her eyes as

she spoke, she was not used to being repri-
manded, or having her work belittled by her
mentor. Madame Markova had always been
so proud of her, and now it was obvious
that she wasn't. The mistress of the ballet
was furious with her.

"You have been working hard. But not
hard enough. You are working without soul,
without spirit. I have always told you that
unless you are willing to give it every ounce
of blood and soul and love and heart you
have, you will be nothing. Don't bother
dancing. Sell flowers on the street, clean
toilets somewhere, you will be more useful.
Nothing is worse than a dancer who gives
nothing."

"I am trying, Madame. I was away for a
long time. I'm not yet as strong as I was."
The tears flowed down her cheeks as she
said it, but Madame Markova showed no
emotion other than disdain and anger. She
looked as though she felt she had been
cheated by Danina.

"It is your heart I am talking about.
Your soul. Not your legs. Your legs will
come back. Your heart will not, if you have
left it somewhere else. You must make a

choice, Danina. It is always a choice here. Unless you want to be like the others. You never were. You were different. You cannot have both. You cannot have a man, or men, and be a truly great prima. And no man is worth your career . . . no man is worth the ballet. In the end, they will always disappoint you. Just as you are disappointing me now, and cheating yourself. You have come back to me with nothing. You are a shell, a nobody, a little dancer in the corps de ballet. You are no longer a prima." It was the cruelest blow of all and almost broke Danina's heart to hear it.

"That's not true. I still have what I did before, I just need to work harder."

"You have forgotten how to. You do not care anymore. Something has come into your life that you love more than ballet. I can see it, I can smell it. Your dancing is pathetic." Just listening to her made Danina's skin crawl, and as she looked into the other woman's eyes, she knew that she had no secrets from her. "It's a man, isn't it? Who did you fall in love with? What man is worth this? Does he even want you?

You are a fool if you sacrifice everything for him."

There was a long moment of silence between them, while Danina weighed her words and how much to tell her. "He is a very good person," she said finally, "and we love each other."

"You are a whore now, like the others, the little cheap ones who dance and play, and to whom it means nothing. You should be dancing on the streets in Paris, not here at the Maryinsky. You don't belong here. I always told you, you cannot be like them if you truly want this. You must choose, Danina."

"I can't give up my whole life forever, Madame, no matter how much I love dancing. I want to do the right thing, I want to be great, I want to be fair to you . . . but I also love him."

"Then you should leave now. Don't waste my time, or that of your teachers. No one wants you here unless you are what you were before. Nothing less is worth it. You must choose, Danina. And if you choose him, you will be making the wrong decision.

I guarantee it. He will never give you what we do. You will never feel about yourself as you do on the stage, knowing you have given a performance that no one will ever forget. That's who you were when you left here. Now you're nothing more than a little dancer."

She couldn't believe what she was hearing, except that the words were familiar. She had heard Madame Markova's point of view before. To her it was a sacred religion one sacrificed one's life for. She had, and she expected everyone else to do it. And Danina always had, but now she couldn't. She wanted her life to be more than just the perfect performance.

"Who is this man?" she asked finally. "Does it even matter?"

"It matters to me, Madame," Danina said respectfully, still believing she could do both, finish well and honorably here, and go to Nikolai when he was ready for her.

"What does he want to do with you?"

"Marry me," Danina said in a whisper, as Madame Markova looked disgusted.

"Then why are you here?" It was too

complicated to explain and she really didn't want to.

"I wanted to finish properly with you, maybe even for the next year, if you want me, if I work hard enough and improve again."

"Why bother?" And then her eyes narrowed suspiciously, and she proved once again to Danina that she was as all-knowing as Danina had always thought her. "Is he already married?"

Again, another long silence between them as Danina did not answer.

"You're a bigger fool than I ever thought you. Worse than one of those little whores. Most of them get husbands at least, and fat, and babies. They are worth nothing. You are wasting your talent on a man who already has a wife. It makes me sick to think of what you are doing, and I don't want to know anything more about it. I want you to work now, Danina, as you used to, as you're capable of, as you owe me, and in two months, I want you to tell me that it is over, and you know that this is your life, and always will be. You must sacrifice everything for it, Danina . . . everything . . . and only then is it worth it, only then will you know true love. This is your love, your only love. This man is nonsense. He means nothing to you. He will only hurt you. I want to hear nothing more about this. Go back to work now," she said, with a wave of dismissal that was so direct and so uncompromising that Danina immediately left her office and went back to class, trembling from what Madame Markova had said to her.

That was the kind of sacrifice she expected, she wanted her to give up everything, even Nikolai, and Danina couldn't. She didn't want to. She didn't owe them that. They had no right to expect it of her. She didn't want to be one of the insane zealots who had no life other than the ballet. She could see that now. She didn't want to be Madame Markova when she was sixty, and have no other life, no children, no husband, no memories, except performances that strung out over the years, and eventually meant nothing.

She had tried to explain it to Nikolai, to tell him what they expected of her, and he hadn't believed her. This *was* what they wanted. Her soul, and her promise that she would end it with him. But she would not do that now, no matter what it cost her. And her anger over it made her work even harder, in class, and at the barre. She began warming up at four o'clock every morning, and stayed until ten o'clock at night, working after classes. She never ate, never stopped, never slept, never did anything but drive her body beyond its utmost limits. It was what they wanted of her, and she looked thin and drawn and exhausted two weeks later when Madame Markova called her into her office once again.

Danina couldn't imagine what she was going to say to her now. Perhaps ask her to leave that morning, but perhaps that would be a relief. She couldn't drive herself any harder, and she hadn't heard a word from Nikolai in three weeks now, and it was driving her insane. He had answered none of her letters, but suddenly she wondered if they had even been mailed. She had left them in the front hall, as she always did, with the others. But perhaps they were being singled out now for the garbage. She was wondering about it as she went to Madame Markova's office, and gave a huge start when she saw him sitting there. It was Nikolai, and he seemed to be having a pleasant conversation with Madame Markova. And when Danina entered the room, he turned to her and smiled. Just seeing him there, she felt her heart pound, and her legs go weak.

"What are you doing here?" she asked, with a look of amazement. She wondered if he had been telling the whole story to Madame Markova, but she understood instantly from the look in his eyes that he hadn't given away their secret. He understood that much, and he was quick to explain his presence to her, or the pretext he had come on, so Danina herself wouldn't make a mistake in what she said in front of Madame Markova.

"I came to see how you are doing, Miss Petroskova, by order of the Czar himself. He wished to be reassured as to your health, since no one has heard anything from you since you left us. The Czarina was particularly worried." He said it with a warm smile at Madame Markova, who had the grace to look a trifle awkward, and briefly turned away.

"Have you not gotten my letters? Have none of you?" Danina looked horrified as he shook his head. "I have been leaving them to be mailed, as I always do. Perhaps they're not mailing my letters." Madame Markova was staring at her desk and said nothing.

"And your health then? You look quite pale, and much thinner than when you left us. I fear you've been working too hard, Danina. Have you? You must not overdo it so soon after being so ill."

"She must retrain her body," Madame Markova said sharply, "and learn discipline again. Her body has forgotten nearly everything she knew." Danina knew as well as her mentor did that that wasn't true. But Nikolai looked worried.

"I'm sure she'll find her old strength again very soon," he said pleasantly, "but she still must not overdo it. I'm sure you're aware of that, Madame Markova," he said with a smile, looking very official and deeply concerned. "And now, may I spend a moment with my patient? I have a private

message for her from the Czar and Czarina." It was impossible to argue with that,
and despite a look of vast displeasure from
Madame Markova, Nikolai and Danina
were allowed to leave her office together. It
was obvious that she was suspicious of him,
but she was not entirely certain he was at
the root of Danina's betrayal either, and
she did not dare accuse him of it. Instead,
she let them go quietly, and Danina led him
downstairs to the small garden. It was still
cool outside, and she put a shawl around
her shoulders, over her leotard. He was
worried to see her looking so thin and tired,
and he longed to put his arms around her
and hold her.

"Are you all right?" he whispered as
they sat alone in the small garden. "I miss
you . . . and I was so worried when I
didn't hear from you."

"They must be throwing away my letters. I'll mail them myself from now on,"
though God only knew when they would
give her enough free time to do it. "What
has happened?" she asked, looking worried,
but still smiling at him. She was so happy to
see him. "Are you all right, Nikolai?"

"Of course . . . Danina, I love you. . . ." He looked anguished as he said it. The pain of her absence had been almost more than he could bear.

"I love you too," she whispered, as their hands clasped tightly, and unseen by them, from an upstairs window, Madame Markova was watching them, but she could not hear what they said. But she saw the two hands tightly clenched, which confirmed her suspicions. Her mouth was set in a thin, angry line of contempt and determination. "Have you told Marie yet?"

His brows knit before he answered, and he nodded. "A few days after you left." But he didn't look pleased with the outcome. Danina could see that at once, and she frowned as she listened.

"What did she say?" It had been a ghastly exchange, and a raging battle ever since then. But he had no intention of losing this one.

"You will never believe it, Danina. She does not want to go back to England. She wants to stay in Russia. After fifteen years of threatening to leave, and telling me how much she hates it here, she will not leave

now, when I am offering to free her."
Danina looked vastly disappointed by what
he told her, and had to fight back tears as
she listened.

"And the divorce?"

"She does not want it. She sees no reason why we should leave each other. She
admits that she's as unhappy as I am, but
she says she doesn't care about happiness in
marriage anymore. She says she does not
want the humiliation of a divorce. And if we
live together now, you and I, I cannot marry
you, Danina." He looked devastated by
what he told her. He had wanted to give her
everything, a home, respectability, security,
children, a whole new life. But all he could
offer her now was to be his mistress. It was
she who would be humiliated now, and not
his wife.

"Does anyone know about us? The
Czar?" Danina asked, looking worried.

"I think he suspects about us, but I
don't think he disapproves. He genuinely
likes you, and has made a point of saying so
to me more than once."

"Don't worry about all this," Danina
said with a sigh. "It will work out in time. I

must finish here anyway. They are very unhappy with me for staying away for so long,
and Madame Markova is threatening to put
me in the corps de ballet, and no longer
allow me to dance as a prima. She says I no
longer dance as I did before. I would like to
come back to where I was when I left, and
that will give you time to convince Marie to
listen to reason. We can be patient." She
tried valiantly to sound calmer than she
was, about her life in the ballet, and about
him.

"I'm not sure I can be patient," he said
unhappily. "I miss you unbelievably. When
can you come back to visit again?" The days
without her had been intolerable for him,
far more than he had feared they would be.

"Perhaps this summer, if they let me
have a break this year. Madame Markova is
talking about making me stay here to work
by myself when the others go on vacation,
to make up for the time I missed when I
was with you."

"Can she do that? That's not fair." He
looked outraged. He wanted her with him.

"She can do anything she wants. Nothing is fair here. We'll see. I'll talk to her

about it when the time is closer. Right now, we must be patient and wait." He wanted more time to talk to Marie anyway, to try and reason with her, and at least get her to leave for England, or agree to some kind of separation.

"I'll come back and see you in a few weeks, 'by order of the Czar.' " He smiled at her. "Will you get the letters if I write to you?"

"Perhaps if you put them in an Imperial envelope," she said with a mischievous look, which made him smile.

"I'll have Alexei address them for me." And then, without saying more, he leaned over and kissed her. "Don't worry, my love. We'll work it all out. They cannot keep us apart forever. We just need some time to find the best solutions. But not too much time. I can't bear being without you for too long." He was about to kiss her again, and as he leaned toward her, they saw the door open to the garden, and Madame Markova was glaring at them.

"Do you intend to spend the entire day with your *doctor*, Danina? Or working? Perhaps you should be in a hospital, if you're still so ill, and the Czar is still so worried about you. I'm sure we can find a good state hospital for you, if you prefer it to dancing here." Danina was already on her feet and standing beside Nikolai in her leotard and her toe shoes, and he spoke before she could.

"I'm very sorry, Madame, if I have taken too much of Miss Petroskova's time. It was not my intention. I was simply concerned."

"Good day then, Dr. Obrajensky." All her gratitude to him for saving Danina five months before had long since been dispelled, particularly now that she knew he was the enemy that she was facing for Danina. She no longer had any doubt about it.

He kissed Danina on the cheek before he left, and she reminded him to give everyone her love, and with a last squeeze of his hand, she went back to class as he left the garden. He looked bereft when he left the building where she ate and slept, and worked and slaved, for eighteen hours a day. He only wished he could take her with him instead of having to leave her there.

And in class once more, she was desperately trying to concentrate and not think of him, as Madame Markova watched her. She was relentless in her vigilance, her criticism, her brutally unkind words. And when Danina finally took a break two hours later, Madame Markova looked at her with undisguised disdain, and met her eyes with disapproval and something very close to rage.

"So, did he tell you that he cannot leave his wife? That she will not agree to a divorce? You're a fool, Danina Petroskova, it is an old, old story. And he will keep making you promises and breaking them, until he breaks your heart and costs you your life as a dancer, and he will never leave her." She sounded as though she spoke from experience, or something very bitter which had touched her a long time ago. She had neither forgiven nor forgotten, nor would she now. "Is that what he told you?" The older woman pressed her, but Danina would never admit to her that it was. She knew that Nikolai would never hurt her, no matter what Madame Markova thought of him, or what demons haunted her from the past.

"He had a message for me from the Czar and Czarina," Danina said calmly.

"And what is that?" Danina did not tell her that they wanted her back for a visit that summer. That would have been the final blow between her and Madame Markova. And she knew she couldn't tell her yet.

"Only that they miss me and are worried about my health."

"How kind of them, what important friends you have now. But they will not help you when you can no longer dance, they will not want you then, and your doctor will forget you long before that." She said it with a bitterness Danina had never seen in her before.

"Not necessarily, Madame," Danina said with quiet dignity, turned on her heel, and went to her next class. There was only so much she would take from her now, and it did not matter to her that Marie would not agree to divorce him or leave for England. They could still have a life together. She was still willing to be with him, married or not.

From then on, every day in May was an

agony, made worse by Madame Markova's constant criticism and accusations. Danina was accused of being out of step, out of time, her arabesques were a disgrace, her arms now moved like wood, her legs were stiff, her leaps pathetic. Madame Markova was doing everything she could to push Danina to breaking point, and break her spirit. She wanted to make her fight for her dancing, and to give up everything but that.

But in spite of it, Danina held on, and Nikolai came to see her again in June. And this time he brought a personal letter from the Czarina. They wanted her to come to Livadia in August, for the entire month if possible, but Danina did not see how she could do it. Nothing had changed with Nikolai in the past month. If anything, Marie was more adamant about staying where she was, and she was making things very difficult about the children, which seemed to surprise him even more.

"I think people do that. They have to make things more painful. Like Madame Markova with me now. It is their own special kind of revenge because in your spirit you have escaped them. And if the Czarina truly wants me to come, she will have to order Madame Markova to send me. She will not dare refuse an Imperial command, otherwise I will not be allowed to accept their invitation, and can't go."

"They can't do that to you," he complained. "You're not a slave here."

"I might as well be," she said, looking exhausted. But when he left this time, he promised that he would have the Czar himself command her to come, if that was what was required.

And this time, when he went back, he made a clean breast of it to the Czar. He told him everything, and begged for his assistance in getting Danina to Livadia. The Czar was moved by what he said, and promised to do what he could, though from what he knew of the ballet, he knew how rigorous it was and how demanding they were of their top dancers.

"They may not even listen to me," he said with a smile. "They think they answer only to God, and I'm not even sure they follow His orders." The Czar smiled at Nikolai.

But the letter that came to Madame

Markova in July was difficult for even her to ignore. The Czar explained that the health of the Czarevitch depended on it, as he had become inordinately attached to Danina, and was inconsolable in her absence. He begged Madame Markova to allow Danina to join them.

And when Danina was called into her office this time, Madame Markova's eyes were blazing and her mouth was set in a hard thin line, and she said only that she would be accompanying Danina to Livadia for a month. They were to leave on the first of August, and Madame Markova looked anything but pleased about it. But that was not what Danina wanted to hear, and she was willing to fight for what she got now. She had worked hard for them for three months, almost to the point of persecution. And now they owed her time away with Nikolai. It was all she wanted of her, and Danina would settle for nothing less.

"No, Madame," she said, taking the older woman completely by surprise. But she sounded like a grown woman now, and no longer an obedient child.

"You will not go?" Madame Markova

looked stunned. The battle was won then, and a slow smile began to dawn in her eyes for the first time since Danina had returned to them. Danina had been a traitor in her eyes since April. "You do not wish to see him?" It was music to her ears, the war had been won more easily than she had dared to hope.

"No. I wish to go alone. You have no reason to come with me. I do not need a chaperone, Madame, although I appreciate your offer to join me. I am quite comfortable with the Imperial family now, and I believe they wish me to come alone." In fact, there had been no mention of Madame Markova in the invitation, and they both knew it.

"I will not let you go without me," Madame Markova said with blazing eyes.

"Then I will explain to the Czar that I am not able to follow his orders." Danina faced her off with a look of determination Madame Markova had never previously seen in her, and she was more displeased than ever, as the smile faded from her face, and she stood up with a look of ice.

"Very well then. You may go for one

month. But I will not promise you that you will still be a prima when we open with *Giselle* in September. Think about it carefully, Danina, before you take that risk."

"I have nothing to think about, Madame. If that is your decision, I will abide by it." But they both also knew that she was dancing better than ever. She had regained all her old strength and skill, and even added some new and far more difficult techniques to it. She had blended maturity with discipline and talent, and the results of her work and growth could not be ignored.

"We begin rehearsals on September first, as you know. Be here on the last day of August," was all Madame Markova said to her and then she stormed out of the office, leaving Danina alone.

Two weeks later, Danina was on the train, unchaperoned, on her way to Livadia, contemplating the friend she had lost in her mentor. She knew for certain now that Madame Markova would never forgive her for her betrayal of the ballet. She had never spoken a single word to Danina before she left, and purposely avoided her when Danina went to say good-bye to her. The friendship between them was over, and only because she was in love with Nikolai. But Danina would do nothing to lose him, or an opportunity to be with him. Nothing was more important to her than that. Not even the ballet.

# Chapter 6

*T*he time that Danina and Nikolai spent together in Livadia was idyllic. They were given a small, discreet guest cottage where he lived with her, openly this time, and they were treated as husband and wife by both the Czar and Czarina. They seemed to understand.

The weather was beautiful, the children were thrilled to see her again, and true to his word, Alexei even "taught" her to swim, and Nikolai helped "a little."

The only thing he regretted now was that she had not met his sons. But that was not possible for now. Marie had still not agreed to the divorce, but at least she had gone to visit her father in Hampshire for the summer, and taken the boys with her.

Nikolai was hoping that being there would remind her of how much she loved it, and wanted to live there, but thus far he was not too optimistic about a change of heart. She seemed to have every intention of staying married to him, if only to torment him.

"It doesn't matter, my love. We are happy like this, aren't we?" Danina reminded him when they spoke of it. They were so happy sharing their little cottage. She had breakfast alone with him every day, on their terrace, and the rest of their meals they took with the family. They were with them all the time, and then shared long, passionate nights alone.

"I want to give you more than a borrowed cottage by the grace of the Czar," Nikolai said mournfully one day, hating Marie more than ever for not giving him his freedom.

"We will have more one day, and I can continue dancing for as long as I have to." More than Nikolai, she was resigned to her fate. But he worried about her.

"That woman is going to kill you if you stay at the ballet much longer," he complained. He was no fonder of Madame

Markova than she was of him. And ever since Danina had returned to the ballet four months before, she looked thinner than ever, and she had been exhausted when she arrived from St. Petersburg. It was inhuman how hard she worked.

This time, she was careful to exercise extensively every day so she didn't lose any of her muscle tone while she was in Livadia, and Alexei loved to watch her dance and practice for hours. The Czarina had someone set up a barre for her, and after she exercised, she went on long walks with Nikolai. She was in perfect shape when the month came to an end, but after another idyllic month together, she couldn't bear the thought of leaving him again.

"We can't go on like this forever," she said sadly, "only seeing each other for a few minutes once a month when you visit. I don't mind having to dance, but I can't bear being away from you." And there would be no more vacations in sight for her now, until Christmas. The Imperial family had already invited her to spend it with them at Tsarskoe Selo, with Nikolai. She could even have her old cottage, to share with him. But that was nearly four months away, and Danina couldn't bear the thought of all she'd have to go through now to get there. It would be four months of hell at Madame Markova's hands, while she was punished for loving a man more than the ballet. It was an insane way to live.

"I want you to stop dancing at Christmas," Nikolai finally said on their last night together. "We'll find a way to work it out somehow. Perhaps you can teach ballet to the Grand Duchesses, or some of the ladies in waiting. And perhaps I can find you a small cottage near the palace, so you can be near me." It was their only hope, if Marie would not agree to divorce him.

"We'll see," she said patiently. "You must not jeopardize your entire life for me. If Marie makes too much of it, she could make trouble for you with the Czar, or cause a terrible scandal. You don't need that."

"I'll talk to her about it again when she comes back from England, and then I'll come to see you."

But as soon as Danina left for St. Petersburg, Alexei fell ill, and Nikolai was needed daily, hourly, for the next six weeks. It was mid-October when he finally was able to see her. By then, Madame Markova kept her as the prima, much to Danina's relief, and she had danced in *Giselle*, as promised.

But Nikolai had nothing but bad news when he came this time. Alexei was still ill, though slightly better now, just enough for his doctor to leave for a few hours, and two of the Grand Duchesses had come down with influenza, which had also kept him very busy. Danina thought he looked very tired, and sad, although he was obviously happy to see her.

Marie had returned from England two weeks before, and was more adamant than ever that she wouldn't free him. She had begun to hear rumors about Danina, and was threatening to create a huge stir, which could cost him his position, or even any remote association with the Czar and Czarina. In fact, Marie was blackmailing him and holding him hostage, and when he had asked her why, she said he owed it to her to treat her respectably and not embarrass her or their sons, although she admitted that she had never loved him. But she was going to hang on to him at all costs now. She said she found it embarrassing to be left for another woman, particularly a ballerina. She said it as though Danina were a prostitute, and it had enraged him. They had argued endlessly, but he got nowhere with her. And he was very depressed about it, which Danina could easily see.

He came again in November, and Madame Markova almost didn't let him see her, but he was so insistent that she finally ran out of excuses. But she only allowed Danina half an hour with him, due to rehearsals. Their only comfort then was knowing that they would be together for three weeks over Christmas and New Year's. For now, it was all they lived for.

He came to all her performances after that, or as many as he was able to attend. And her father came to one as well, as he did each year, but unfortunately they were never at the same performance, so she couldn't introduce Nikolai to her father.

But tragedy struck her family the week before Christmas. Her youngest and favorite brother was killed in Molodechno on the Eastern Front during a battle, and she was in deep mourning for him during her last performance, and still in a somber mood when Nikolai came to take her back to her little guest cottage at Tsarskoe Selo, and he was deeply solicitous of her loss. Knowing her brother was gone now pained her deeply, and even Alexei thought she looked very sad, and much quieter than usual, as he reported to his parents, after he visited Danina just after she arrived.

But Christmas with them was magical, and her spirits rose as she spent time with Nikolai, talking quietly, exchanging books as they had before. He stayed with her openly, as he had at Livadia that summer. They talked about how much they loved each other, and the good times they had shared, but there was little they could say now about their future. Marie had remained entrenched in her unreasonable and immobile position. But he had nonetheless begun to look at small houses for Danina, and was determined to save up enough money to buy one so she could give up dancing, and come to live with him. But they both knew that it would take time, perhaps even a great deal of it, before either of them could afford it. She had promised herself, and him, that she would dance through the spring now, and perhaps until the end of the year.

But as soon as she returned to the ballet this time, she began feeling ill. She ate even less than before, and when he saw her at the end of January, he was seriously dismayed by the way she looked, and how pale she was.

"You're working too hard," he complained, as usual, but more stridently this time. "Danina, they're going to kill you, if you don't stop."

"You can't die of dancing." She smiled, hating to admit to him how ill she felt. She didn't want to worry him, with Marie being so difficult, and the Czarevitch sick again. Nikolai had enough problems to concern him, without adding her health to the rest. But she was growing dizzier by the day, and had nearly fainted twice in class, though she said nothing to anyone, and no one seemed to notice how miserable she felt. By February, she felt so ill that she was actually unable to get out of bed one morning.

She forced herself to dance that afternoon anyway, but when Madame Markova saw her, Danina was sitting on a bench with her eyes closed, and she was looking gray.

"Are you ill again?" Madame Markova asked in an accusing tone, still unwilling and unable to forgive her for her continuing affair with the Czar's young doctor. She made no attempt to hide the fact that she thought it a disgrace, and had distanced herself from Danina.

"No, I'm fine," Danina said weakly. But Madame Markova followed her with worried eyes all through the next days, and this time when Danina nearly fainted in a rehearsal late one night, Madame Markova saw it instantly and came to her aid.

"Shall I call a doctor for you?" She asked more gently this time. In truth, Danina was giving them all she ever had and more, but it was no longer enough to satisfy the debt Madame Markova felt she owed them. She had been merciless with her, but seeing how ill Danina was, even she relented. "Do you want me to send for Dr. Obrajensky?" she asked, much to Danina's dismay.

Danina would have liked nothing better than to have an excuse to see him, but she didn't want to frighten him, and she felt sure that she was very ill. It was more than a year since she had had influenza. But in the ten months since she had returned to the ballet she had pushed herself so relentlessly that she began to think she had destroyed her health, just as Nikolai had warned. Her head swam constantly, she could no longer eat anything without becoming violently ill, and she was exhausted. She could barely put one foot in front of the other, yet she was dancing sixteen and eighteen hours a day, and every night when she went to bed, she felt as though she would die in her bed. Perhaps Nikolai had been right after all, she thought one night as she lay in bed, wanting to vomit and not having the strength to get up again to do it. Perhaps the ballet was going to kill her after all.

Five days later, she was unable to get out of bed, and she felt so ghastly, she didn't care what Madame Markova did to her, or who she called. All Danina wanted to do was lie there and die. She was only sorry she wouldn't see Nikolai again, and wondered who would tell him when she was gone.

She was lying with her eyes closed, drifting out of consciousness, as the room spun slowly around each time she opened her eyes, when she dreamed that she saw him, standing beside her bed. She knew he couldn't be there, and wondered if she was delirious again, as she had been with the influenza. She even heard him speaking to her, and calling her name, and then she saw him turn and say something to Madame Markova, asking her why he hadn't been called sooner.

"She did not want me to call you," she heard a vision of Madame Markova say, and then she opened her eyes again to see him. Even if the vision wasn't real, she thought, it looked just like Nikolai. She felt his hand on hers then, as he took her pulse, and he bent very near her and asked her if she could hear him. All she could do was nod, she felt too ill to speak anymore.

"We must get her to a hospital," the vision said very clearly. But she had no fever this time.

He did not yet know what was wrong with her, except that she had been so ill, and hadn't been able to hold anything down, not water or food, in so many days that she actually appeared to be dying. As he looked at her, his eyes filled with tears.

"You have literally worked her to death, Madame," he said in barely controlled fury, "and you will answer to me if she dies, and to the Czar," he added for good measure. And as Danina listened to him speak, she realized that he was real, and this time she wasn't dreaming. It really was Nikolai.

"Nikolai?" she said weakly, as he took her hand in his again, and whispered as he bent close to her.

"Don't talk, my love, try to rest. I'm here now." He was standing next to her and they were talking about hospitals and an ambulance, and she was trying to tell him that she didn't need one. It all seemed like too much trouble. She just wanted to lie in her bed and die, with Nikolai there near her, holding her hand.

He sent everyone away, and examined her quietly, remembering the graceful body with longing. He hadn't been with her for two months now, and nothing had changed. He was as much in love with her as ever, but for the moment the ballet still owned her, as Marie did him. He was beginning to wonder, as was Danina, if they'd ever be together, or if it would always be this way.

"What has been happening to you? Can you tell me, Danina?"

"I don't know . . . sick all the time . . ." she mumbled, drifting off to sleep as she talked to him, and then waking again, feeling desperately ill and retching. But her stomach was long since empty. She was beyond bile now. All she had were the dry heaves, as she had had for days. It was easier not to eat or drink at all, so she wouldn't be vomiting every moment. And she was still dancing sixteen hours a day, forcing herself to go on, until she could do no more.

"Danina, talk to me," he insisted, waking her again. He was beginning to worry that she was going to slip into a coma, from starvation, dehydration, and sheer exhaustion. They were working her to death, literally, and her body seemed to be giving up

from the constant pressure, and lack of anything to sustain it. "What are you feeling?
How long have you been this way?" He was
growing frantic, and they were still waiting
to hear if he wanted to take her to the
hospital or needed an ambulance. He still
wasn't sure, but he was growing more
frightened by the way she looked.

"How long have you felt this way?" he
asked again. She hadn't been this bad when
he last saw her, although she hadn't looked
well, and she had admitted to him even
then that she hadn't been feeling well lately.

"A month . . . two months . . ." she
said, sounding groggy.

"Have you been vomiting for that
long?" He looked horrified. How long had
it been since she'd had proper nourish-
ment? And how long could she survive it?
He thanked God that Madame Markova
had finally called him. In the end, she was
afraid not to, given Danina's indirect con-
nection to the Czar. Besides, despite her
rage at her for the past year, in truth, Madame Markova loved her, and even she was
terrified by what she saw. "Danina . . .
talk to me. . . . When did this start? Ex-

actly. Try and remember." Nikolai pressed her, as Danina opened her eyes, and tried to remember how long she had been ill. It seemed like forever to her.

"January. When I came back from Christmas vacation." It was nearly two months now. But all she wanted to do was sleep, and she wanted him to stop talking to her.

"Do you have pain anywhere?" He was gently feeling all over her body, but she complained of nothing. She was just desperately weak, and malnourished. She had been literally starving. He thought of her appendix, but there was no sign of infection to show for it, or a bleeding ulcer, but she insisted she had not been vomiting blood or anything dark and ominous, when he asked her. There were no symptoms except that she had vomited endlessly and was now barely conscious, and too weak to move. He didn't even dare take her to the hospital until he knew more about it. He didn't think she had either tuberculosis or typhoid, although the former was not impossible, in which case she would already be in the final stages. But he didn't think so.

He listened to her lungs, her heart. Her pulse was weak, but he could not understand what he was seeing. And then he asked her a question he knew she would think indelicate, but he was not only her lover, he was a doctor, and he needed to know. But her answer to that did not surprise him either. Her system was so entirely depleted, and she danced so much, so long, and so hard, it was not unusual to have a cessation of all female functions, and then suddenly he thought of something else. They had always been careful . . . always . . . except after Christmas. Only once. Or twice.

He looked her over carefully again, and then he knew with a sinking heart, and with a gentle hand he felt low on her abdomen and touched a small, barely palpable lump, but it was just big enough to tell him what he hadn't even suspected. She was almost certainly two months pregnant, and she had so brutalized herself, and been so ill, and worked so hard, that she might well have died from it. And if she was pregnant, in the condition she was in, it was a miracle she hadn't lost the baby.

"Danina," he whispered to her when she woke up again, and looked at him questioningly, "I think you're pregnant." He said it so softly that he knew no one would hear him, but her eyes widened instantly in surprise. She had thought of it once or twice and then dismissed it from her mind entirely. It could not be. She could not let herself think of it. But as he said it, she knew it, and closed her eyes again, as a tear trickled from the corner of her eyes.

"What will we do now?" she whispered back, looking at him in despair. This truly would destroy both their lives, and Marie would never release him, if only out of vengeance.

"You must come back with me. You can live in the cottage until you're feeling stronger." But it was only a temporary solution, and they both knew it. They had far bigger problems now.

"And then what?" Danina said sadly. "I cannot go to live with you . . . you can't marry me . . . the Czar will take your position away . . . we can't afford a house yet . . . and I can't dance for much longer if you're right." But she knew he was. Some girls had danced for as long as they could, and they were always found out after a month or two, and banished. Some lost their babies from the long hours and grueling rehearsals. She knew that. There was no easy answer for her now.

"We'll work it out together," he said, desperately worried about her. He couldn't even give her a place to live, let alone a place to bring their baby. But he couldn't think of anything sweeter than a child born of their love. Yet there seemed to be no place and no way to have it. And how would they support it once she stopped dancing? Their savings were pitifully small, and she earned more praise than money. And Marie and the boys used every penny he made. "We'll think of something," he said gently. But she only shook her head and cried softly as he held her. She seemed overwhelmed with despair. "Let me take you back with me," he said, looking anxious. "No one need know why you're ill. We have to talk about it." But she knew better than anyone that there was nothing to talk about and nothing to hope for. All their dreams were still far in the future, with no way to attain them.

"I have to stay here," she said, and the thought of going anywhere made her feel even sicker. This time she could not go with him. But he hated to leave her, especially knowing what he did now.

He stayed with her until late that night, and told Madame Markova he feared a serious ulcer, and he said that he thought that she should return to the cottage at the palace until she was better. But it was Danina who fought him, and told Madame Markova that she didn't want to leave, she felt too ill, and she could get well here just as quickly as at the cottage, which wasn't true, they all knew. But Madame Markova was pleased that she didn't want to go with him. She thought it a hopeful sign that the affair with Nikolai might be ending. It was the first time Danina had resisted anything he said.

"We are perfectly capable of caring for her here, Doctor, though perhaps not as elegantly as at Tsarskoe Selo," she said with an edge of sarcasm, and Nikolai was distraught that Danina would not agree to go with him. He argued with her endlessly after Madame Markova left them.

"I want you with me. I want to take care of you, Danina. You must come."

"For how long? Another month? Two? And then what?" she said miserably. She knew there was only one solution, but she did not mention it to him. She knew other girls in the ballet who had done it and survived it. She wanted nothing more than his baby too, but they had no hope of having it. Maybe later, but not in the circumstances they were still in. They had to face that, and she wasn't sure Nikolai was ready to admit it. In fact, she was sure he wasn't. He was far too worried about her. "You must leave me, Nikolai," she said. "You can come back in a few days."

"I'll come back tomorrow," he said, and left feeling desperately worried about her, and panicked about her situation. They had only been careless once or twice, but it was the last thing he had expected to happen. And now he had to help her find a solution. This was his fault, he knew, more than hers. And he was agonized that

Danina was paying the price more than he was.

But when he returned the next day, neither of them had any simple answers. They could not afford, or take care of, a baby. They couldn't even afford a place to live. It simply wasn't possible, she knew, though he insisted it was, but Danina didn't argue with him. She just lay there miserably, crying silently, and continuing to retch and vomit. He was forcing her to eat now, and drink what she could, and she seemed a little stronger to him, but she was so violently ill, she felt worse rather than better. He was in tears too, as he sat helplessly by and watched her. He knew she'd feel better in a month or two. But in the meantime, she was going through torture.

And when he left again, she went to talk to one of the other dancers. Danina knew for certain that the girl she spoke to, Valeria, had done it, twice, from what she had heard. Valeria told her where to go and who to talk to, and even offered to go with her, and Danina gratefully accepted her assistance.

The two girls left the next morning, as

quietly as they could, when the others went to church. It was Sunday, and Madame Markova was at church, as she was every Sunday. Danina was obviously too ill to go, and Valeria had feigned a migraine headache. They left hurriedly, with Danina getting sick every five minutes on the way. They had to walk halfway across town, but eventually they got to the address in a poor neighborhood with filth everywhere around them.

It was a small, dark house, with dirty curtains in the window, and the look of the woman who opened the door made Danina shudder, but Valeria promised it would be over quickly and done well. Danina had brought all her savings with her, and hoped she had enough money. She had been horrified when she heard how much it would cost her.

The woman who called herself a "nurse" asked Danina a series of questions. She wanted to be sure it hadn't gone too far, but two months didn't seem to worry her. And after taking half her money from her, she led Danina into a bedroom in the back. The sheets and blankets looked dirty, and there were bloodstains on the floor, which no one had bothered to clean up after the last visitor had come to see "the nurse."

The old woman washed her hands in a bowl of water standing in a corner, and she took out a tray of instruments that she said had been washed, but they looked terrifying to Danina, as she turned away from the sight of the old woman.

"My father was a doctor," the nurse explained, but Danina didn't want to hear about it, she just wanted to get it over with, and she knew that if Nikolai knew what she was doing, he would have done anything to stop her, and once he found out, might never forgive her. But she couldn't let herself think of that now. The worst of it was that they both wanted this baby, but she knew they couldn't have it. There was no way they could even think about it, she had to do this for both their sakes, no matter how terrible it was, or even if it killed her in the end. And as she thought about it, and wondered if it would, the nurse told her to take her clothes off, and Danina's hands trembled mercilessly as she did so. And finally she lay on the filthy bed wearing only her sweater, as the woman examined her and nodded her head. Just as Nikolai had, she felt the small, round, tight lump low in her belly.

Nothing that had ever happened to Danina in her life had prepared her for this humiliation and horror. Nothing she had ever known with Nikolai bore any relation to this, and as she thought of it, she began to vomit. But it didn't seem to stop the woman who called herself a nurse, and she assured Danina it would be over soon. The "nurse" told Danina she could stay for a little while until she was strong enough to walk again, and then she had to leave. If there were problems, she was to call a doctor, and not return here. The nurse said she did not handle problems afterward. After her job was done, the rest was on Danina's shoulders. She would not be allowed in if she tried to come back, the woman said to her somewhat darkly.

"Let's get started," the nurse said firmly. She liked getting her patients in and out quickly, before they caused her too much trouble. And the fact that Danina was still vomiting didn't stop her, but Danina asked her to wait for just a minute, and then signaled that she was ready. She was too frightened to speak.

Danina braced herself as the woman told her to, and with one strong arm, she held Danina's leg down, and told her in a stern voice not to move. But Danina's legs were shaking too violently to obey her. And nothing anyone had said had prepared her for the sharp pain she felt as the woman plunged into her with the tool she used. Danina tried not to scream as she looked at the ceiling, or choke on her own vomit as she did. The pain seemed to go on end-lessly, and the room began to spin around her almost instantly, as she finally slipped into merciful blackness. And then suddenly the woman was shaking her, and there was a cold cloth on her head, as the nurse told her she could get up. It was over.

"I don't think I can stand yet," Danina said weakly. The smell of vomit was heavy in the room, and the sight of a pan of blood near the bed nearly made her faint again, as the woman pulled her to her feet and helped her to dress without waiting any longer. Danina was reeling with dizziness and pain and terror as the nurse put rags between her legs. It was all too unbearable to think of as Danina walked slowly into the next room to find her friend, barely able to see her through the dizziness that engulfed her, and she was stunned to realize they had been there less than an hour. Valeria looked worried but relieved. She knew better than anyone how bad it was, having been through it herself.

"Take her home and put her to bed," the nurse said, holding the door open for them, and they were lucky to find a taxi driving past. Later, Danina remembered nothing of the trip back to the ballet. All she remembered was climbing back into her bed, and feeling the rags between her legs, and the searing pain the woman had left inside her. Danina could think of nothing now, not of Nikolai, or their baby, or any part of what had just happened. She simply rolled over in bed with a soft moan, and within seconds, was unconscious.

# Chapter 7

When Nikolai came to see her that afternoon, he found her fast asleep in her bed with her clothes on. He had no idea where she'd been, or what she'd done, so he was relieved at least that she was sleeping, until he looked at her a little closer. Her face was gray, and he noticed her lips were faintly blue, and when he took her pulse, he panicked, and then tried to wake her, and found he couldn't. She was not sleeping, he realized, she was deeply unconscious. And when, out of instinct, if nothing more medical, he pulled her covers back, he saw that she was lying in a pool of blood that had spread all around her. She had been hemorrhaging for hours.

And this time, he did not hesitate for

an instant. He sent one of the dancers for an ambulance, and in terror he began taking her clothes off. She was very nearly dead, and he had no idea how much blood she'd already lost but what he saw around her looked tremendous. And the rags he found between her legs told him the whole story of what had happened.

"Oh my God . . . oh . . . Danina . . ." There was nothing he could do to staunch the flow of blood. She needed surgery, and perhaps even that would not save her. And as soon as she heard, Madame Markova came running to Danina's room. The scene that met her in Danina's small dormitory told her all she needed to know. Nikolai was sitting beside her, holding her hand as tears rolled down his face. And the look of despair he wore touched even Madame Markova. But as the ballet mistress entered the room, Nikolai's sorrow and sense of helplessness turned rapidly to anger. "Who let her do this?" he asked the ballet mistress sharply. "Did you know about it?" His tone was one of accusation, grief, and fury.

"I knew nothing," she said angrily,

"probably even less than you did. She must have gone out when we went to church," she said miserably, afraid for Danina's life.

"How long ago was that?"

"Four or five hours."

"My God . . . don't you understand that this could kill her?"

"Of course I understand that." They wanted to throttle each other in their respective terror for the girl they both loved. But fortunately, the ambulance came quickly, and took her to a hospital Nikolai knew well, and he told them what little he knew of what had happened. She never regained consciousness before surgery, and it was two hours before the surgeon came to see him and Madame Markova, sitting in silence in the barren waiting room, staring at each other.

"How is she?" Nikolai asked quickly, as Madame Markova listened, but the surgeon looked less than pleased. It had very nearly been a disaster, and they were giving her her fourth transfusion.

"If she lives," he said solemnly, "I believe she will still be able to have children. But the outcome is still not certain. She has lost a vast quantity of blood, and whoever did it must have been a butcher." He described the situation medically to Nikolai, and other than the hemorrhaging that refused to stop despite everything they did, they were deathly afraid of infection. "This will not be easy for her," the surgeon explained to Madame Markova. "She must stay here for several weeks, perhaps longer, if she even survives it. We will know more by tomorrow morning, if she lives through the night. For now, we've done all we can for her." Madame Markova was crying softly when the surgeon finished.

"May I see her?" Nikolai asked respectfully, terrified by what the surgeon had said. He would give them no reassurance she would survive.

"You can't do anything for her now," the surgeon explained. "She's still not conscious, and may not be for a while."

"I'd like to be there when she wakes up," Nikolai said quietly, aghast at what had happened, and that he had known nothing about it, and been unable to stop her. They would have worked it out somehow. He had thought about it all night, and turned assorted solutions over in his mind. She didn't have to risk her life to solve the problem. It could all have been worked out, or so he thought.

They let Nikolai into the surgery, where she was still recovering, and she still looked gray to him, in spite of the transfusions she'd been given. He sat down quietly beside her, and took her free hand in his. He held it gently in his own as tears coursed down his cheeks, as he thought of the time they had spent together, and how much he loved her. He would have liked to kill whoever had done this to her. And in the waiting room, Madame Markova was looking devastated and suffering from all the same emotions as he, but they were of no use to each other. Her mentor and her lover were lost in their own thoughts and their own worlds, as Danina struggled for survival.

It was nearly midnight when Danina finally stirred, with a pitiful moan. Her lips were dry, and she could barely open her eyes, but as she turned her head, she saw him, and a sob instantly caught in her throat as she vaguely remembered what had happened, and what she had done to their baby.

"Oh, Danina . . . I'm so sorry. . . ." He cried like a child as he held her in his arms, and begged her to forgive him for putting her in this situation. He didn't even scold her for what she had done. It was too late for that, and she had paid a high price for it. "How could this happen? Why didn't you talk to me before you did it . . . ?"

"I knew . . . you'd never . . . let me . . . do it. . . . I'm so sorry," she cried too. They both did, for each other and their unborn baby. But now all he wanted was for her to get well. He knew, just from looking at her, that it was going to take a long time for her to recover from all that had just happened. But by morning, the surgeon said she was going to make it, and Nikolai had to fight back tears of relief. And out of respect for her, Nikolai went and told Madame Markova, but after she cried, she left without seeing Danina. The surgeon said she was still too ill to see anyone, and Nikolai agreed with him.

He didn't leave her side until that evening, and only then went home to change his clothes and check on Alexei, and make sure that Dr. Botkin was still able to relieve him. He explained that a friend was gravely ill in the hospital, and he needed to be with her. And although his colleague didn't ask, he was certain who it was.

"Will she be all right?" Dr. Botkin asked gently, startled by Nikolai's ravaged face and look of anguish. It had been an agonizing night for him as well, worrying about her.

"I hope so," Nikolai said quietly.

He was back at her side late that night, and sat next to her all night without sleeping, yet again. She drifted in and out of consciousness, muttering, talking to people he couldn't see, and she cried out his name more than once, and begged him to help her. It tore his heart out watching her, but through it all he sat silently, holding her hand, and thinking of their future, and the other children he hoped they would have.

It was two days before the bleeding fully stopped, and the transfusions seemed to begin to help her. She was still too weak to sit up, but he spoon-fed soup and gruel into her, like any nurse, and slept on a cot beside her bed. After seeing her a little better, he finally dared to sleep himself. He was utterly exhausted, but deeply grateful Danina had survived it.

"How do you feel today?" he asked gently, looking at the dark circles beneath her eyes. She still looked ashen to him.

"A little better," she lied. She couldn't remember any of the other girls being so ill in similar situations, although one often heard of women who died from it, but she had had no clear understanding of the risk she was taking. And even if she had, she would have done it anyway. She had absolutely no choice, she felt, and even now, with Nikolai at her side, she knew they could never have had the baby. It would have destroyed everything, his life, her career. There was no room for a child in their lives. They barely had room for each other, no matter how much she loved him. Theirs was a life of stolen moments and borrowed time and only the hope and promise of a future. It was not yet a life in which they could include a child.

"I want you to come back to Tsarskoe

Selo with me," he said as she closed her eyes again, but he knew that this time she could hear him. And her eyes fluttered open again as she listened to what he said. "You can stay at the cottage again. No one has to know why you're ill, or what happened." But even he knew that for a long time she would be too weak to go anywhere, and there was still the risk of infection, which could easily be fatal. He was still deeply concerned about her, as was her surgeon.

"I can't do that again. I can't impose on the Czarina," she said weakly, although she would have liked nothing better than to be with him, as they had been in the cottage before. She loved the sweetness of their living together. But she could not abandon the ballet again to recuperate. She knew that this time Madame Markova would not take her back, or ever forgive her for deserting them, sick or not. Danina had paid a high price with her for her last recuperation, and she needed the ballet. Nikolai could not help her, he was not free to marry her, or care for her, or even able to support her. She had to rely on herself.

"You can't go back to dancing for a while," he said carefully, and then he decided to tell her what he'd been thinking. "I want you to think about something. I have thought of a thousand ways to solve our problem, while you were lying here. We cannot go on this way. Marie will never relent. It will take me years to buy a house for you, and Madame Markova will never release you from the ballet. I want to be with you, Danina. I want us to have a life together, away from all of this, and all the people who want to keep us apart. I want a real life with you, far from here, where we can begin again. We cannot be married, but no one need ever know." And then he added gently, "In another place, we could even have children." A look of sorrow crossed her face as he said the words, and he squeezed her hand. They both felt the loss of what had just happened between them.

"There is no place where we can do that. Where would we go? How would we support ourselves? If Madame Markova wishes to discredit me, no other ballet will have me." She was thinking of Moscow, and other cities in Russia, but he wasn't. His plan was far more daring than that.

"I have a cousin in America. In a place called Vermont. It is in the Northeast, and he says it looks a great deal like Russia. I have enough money saved to pay for our passage there. We can live with him at first. I will find a job, and you can teach ballet somewhere, to little children." She knew Nikolai spoke English perfectly, because of his wife, but she did not. She couldn't imagine a life in a world so far from theirs, and the very thought of it was frightening and foreign to her.

"How could we do that, Nikolai? Could you be a doctor there?" she asked, stunned by the suggestion that she follow him halfway around the world.

"Eventually," he answered carefully. "I would have to go back to school in America. It would take time. I could do other things in the meantime." But what, she asked herself as she listened to him. Shovel snow? Clean stables? Curry horses? To her, the situation seemed hopeless. Surely there was no ballet in Vermont, wherever that was, and that was all she knew. Who would she teach? Who would hire either of them? How would they get there? "You must let me work this out for us. It's our only hope, Danina. We cannot stay here." But to leave required a series of betrayals, abandoning his children and wife, the Czar and his family, who had been so kind to him, and Madame Markova and the Maryinsky Ballet, which was the only home she had known since she was a child. She had given everything to them, her life, her soul, her spirit, her body, and in turn they had given her a life, which was the only one she knew. What would she do in this place called Vermont, and what if he should tire of her and abandon her there? It was the first time she had thought that, but she was frightened, and she looked it, as she met his eyes. And he could easily read all her fears there.

"I don't know. . . . It is so far away. . . . And what if your cousin doesn't want us?"

"He will. He is a kind man. He is older than I, widowed, and he has no children. He has invited me to visit him for years. If I tell him we need his help, he will do it. He has a big house, and some money. He owns

a bank, and he lives alone. He would wel-
come us there. Danina, it is the only hope
we have for a future together. We must begin again somewhere, and forget everything
we have known here." But as much as she
wanted to be with him, she wasn't sure she
could do it. "You mustn't think about it
now. Get healthy and strong, and we will
talk about it again. I will write to him in the
meantime, and see what he says."

"Nikolai, no one would ever forgive
us." The mere thought of it filled her with
terror, and grief.

"And if we stay here? What will we
have? Stolen moments, a few weeks a year
when the Czarina invites you to Livadia or
Tsarskoe Selo? I want a life with you. I want
to wake up beside you every morning, to be
with you when you're ill. . . . I never want
something like this to happen to you
again. . . . Danina, I want our children."
She also wanted the life he described to
her, but they each had to hurt everyone
they had ever loved in order to be free.

"What about my father and brothers?"
She had a family here, a history, a life. She
could not turn her back on all of it because

she loved him. And yet he was willing to do that for her, and he had as much to lose as she did. He had to abandon his children, his wife, and his career in order to be with her.

"You told me yourself you never see your family," he reminded her. And for nearly the past two years, her brothers and father had been at the front. "They would be happy for you." Nikolai did everything he could to convince her. "You cannot dance forever, Danina." But as he said the words to her, she remembered everything Madame Markova had ever said.

"I can teach afterward, like Madame Markova."

"You can teach in Vermont. Perhaps even start a school of your own. I will help you." He seemed so sure, and so strong.

"I must think about it," she said, exhausted by the prospect of such an enormous decision, and all that it entailed.

"Rest now. We will talk about it later." She nodded, and drifted off to sleep again, but she had nightmares of terrifying, unknown places. She kept dreaming of losing Nikolai there, of wandering the streets, looking for him, and never finding him, and when she awoke in the hospital, he was gone, and she was crying and alone. He had left her a note that he had gone to check on Alexei, and would return to see her in the morning. And as she read it, she was lost in thought.

She stayed in the hospital for two weeks, and when she left, the doctor ordered her to stay in bed for two more. Nikolai wanted her to stay at the Czar's cottage with him, at Tsarskoe Selo, but Madame Markova was violently opposed to it. She wanted Danina back at the ballet, and said the trip to Tsarskoe Selo was too far. This time, Danina didn't have the energy to fight her. The mistress of the ballet was too determined, and unwilling, to let Danina slip out of her hands again. She didn't want her to spend another four months "recuperating" in the cottage with her lover. She was intransigent this time, and in the face of the ferocity of her objections, Danina returned to the ballet.

And as Nikolai had when she was ill when they first met, he came to see her every day, and stayed for as long as he could, a few hours at least, before he went back to his own duties. He sat in her dormitory room with her while she rested in bed. And while she walked slowly around the small garden at the ballet with him, he talked to her of Vermont, and his cousin there. He was convinced it was the only way, and he wanted to go with her as soon as they could both get away. He suggested early summer, which was only a few months away.

"Your season will be over then. You can complete what you are doing. We must pick a time, and then go through with it. There will never be a perfect moment to leave, we must seize the moment while we can." She would be twenty-two by then, and he would be forty-one that year, time enough for both of them to start a new life in America, as countless others had done before them, some for reasons as complicated as theirs.

She promised to think about it, and she did, constantly. All she could think about now was the terror of moving to Vermont. Madame Markova sensed easily that something was happening to her. Danina was still tired and pale, and she looked deeply unhappy at times after Nikolai's visits. He was asking her to cast her lot with him, follow him to the end of the world, and trust him completely. And in spite of her love for him, it was a great deal to ask.

"You are troubled, Danina," Madame Markova said cautiously one afternoon, when she came to visit her, and sat beside Danina's bed while she rested. Nikolai had just left her, and as always they had spoken of the same things. Their future. Vermont. His cousin. Leaving Russia. And the ballet. "He is asking you to leave us, isn't he?" she asked wisely, and Danina didn't answer her. She didn't want to lie, or tell her the truth either. "It always happens that way. They fall in love with who you are, and then want to take it away from you," she persisted. "I promise you, Danina, if you leave us, it will kill you. You will be nothing. And when he casts you aside one day for someone more fascinating, or perhaps even younger, you will regret all your life the part of your heart you left here." She made it sound like a death sentence, and it was, in a way. But it was also an exchange for something Danina wanted desperately. It would be the end of her life as a ballerina, but the beginning of her life with Nikolai, a real life with him, which she also wanted. But to have it, she had to sacrifice everything she had now, just as he did. "If he truly loved you, Danina, he would not ask you to leave us."

"And when I am old, what will I have without him, if I stay here?"

"A life you can be proud of in remembering. No one can ever take that from you. Instead of a life of shame, which is all that he can give you. He is a married man, and his wife will not leave him. You will always be his mistress, the little ballet dancer he sleeps with, nothing more."

But there was so much more between them, even now, and Danina knew that. "You make it sound so tawdry, and it isn't," Danina said sadly.

"It is precisely what these things always are. Extremely romantic in the beginning. A dream you think you will have. And when you wake up from it one day, you will find it is a nightmare. *This* is the only life you will ever have that means something to you, this is the life you have worked hard for and trained for. Can you throw it all away for a man who cannot even marry you? Look what has just happened to you. How beautiful was that? How romantic?" It was a cruel thing to say and it unnerved Danina just listening to her. What if she was right? If Nikolai threw her away one day, if she regretted giving up the ballet all her life, and hated Vermont, if they were not happy together? Who could know the answers to those questions? There was no certainty to his plans, only promises, and hopes and dreams, and wishes. Hers as much as his own. Yet he was willing to give up medicine for her, the security he had, the life he had known for over fifteen years with his family. He was willing to sacrifice all for her. Why couldn't she do the same for him?

"You must think about it very carefully," Madame Markova reminded her, "and come to the right decision." The right decision to her, of course, was staying at the ballet and forgetting Nikolai, but Danina also knew she couldn't do that. Leaving the ballet now might destroy her life, but losing him would kill her. Just thinking about it, she felt under the blouse she wore for her locket, and was comforted to feel it there. She was deeply in love with him. Perhaps even enough to risk everything and follow him. Now all she could do was think about it, and look into her heart.

Madame Markova left her alone after that, to her own thoughts. She had planted the seeds she wanted to, and hoped that they would grow and take hold. She wanted Danina to feel the loss and terror of leaving the ballet, of perhaps a lifetime of regret and sorrow. It was certainly something to ponder. It was the only life Madame Markova knew, the only one she ever wanted, it was the legacy she wanted to give Danina now, the sacred bond, the holy grail, the wand passed from hand to hand, from teacher to student to teacher and back again, endlessly, the almost holy vow they took when they came, the love too deep to escape in the end, the sacrifices endless. To stay here now meant giving up all hope of a future with him. In a sense, it meant giving up hope. But to leave Russia with him meant giving up who she was forever. It was an agonizing choice, and whichever road she chose would require sacrifices almost too agonizing to think of. And all Danina could do now was pray that the right answer would come.

# Chapter 8

*D*anina did not dance for a month, and began taking class again on the first of April. There was still snow on the ground outside, and once again she had to work harder than before to regain what she had lost, but this time the return to full strength was swifter. She was stronger now, and in better health.

She was back in rehearsals within a week, and performing again in early May. It was over a year since she had left Nikolai after their long, idyllic stay in the Czar's guest cottage during her convalescence from influenza. And in a year, little had changed between them. They were still deeply in love with each other, he was still married and living with his wife and children, and she was still at the ballet. But they were no closer than they had been a year before to a solution to their problems. If anything, Marie Obrajensky was more firmly entrenched than she had ever been in not leaving him. And in the past year, the two lovers had been able to save very little money for their future together. All they knew for sure was that a life together was still what they wanted. How to achieve it was the obstacle they constantly struggled to overcome. And Danina could not bring herself to agree to join him in Vermont. It was too big a change, she felt, too far away, too unknown, too foreign to her. And Nikolai continued to try and convince her, as gently as he could.

One of the Grand Duchesses fell ill in June, and kept both Imperial physicians busy. Nikolai had little time to visit Danina. He wanted to, but he couldn't get away, and she understood. And in early July, she had another tragedy when her oldest brother was killed in Czernoivitz. She had lost two now, and she knew from his letter that her father was beside himself over the death of his son. He had been with him when they were shelled, and miraculously he had been spared, but his firstborn was killed instantly. Danina took the news hard, and for weeks afterward she felt drained and lifeless. The war was taking a toll on all of them, even at the ballet. Dancers had lost brothers, friends, fathers, and one of their teachers had lost both her sons in April. Even in their cloistered world, it was impossible to ignore the war anymore.

The only thing she had to look forward to that year was another vacation with Nikolai and the Imperial family in Livadia. And this time Madame Markova made no attempt to oppose it. She had come to an uneasy truce with Nikolai after Danina's last illness. She knew that he would have gladly stolen Danina from her, but the young prima showed no sign of going anywhere, or giving up the ballet for him. And Madame Markova felt secure now in her belief that Danina would never be able to bring herself to leave. Just as it was, and always had been to Madame Markova, the ballet was Danina's life.

The Czar was not in Livadia that year, he was with his troops in Mogilev, and felt obliged to stay with them. So it was only the women and children and both physicians who were there, and Danina. The Czarina and her daughters had allowed themselves to take a brief time off from nursing the soldiers, and were happy to be in Livadia again. They were all old friends now, and she and Nikolai were happier than they had ever been. It seemed a perfect time to both of them, a magical moment suspended in time, protected from a dangerous world seemingly far from them. In the safety of Livadia, they were shielded from the realities that had already engulfed everything else.

They had picnics every afternoon, went on long walks, rowed boats and swam, and Danina felt like a child again, as she played the old familiar games with Alexei. His health had been frail that year, and he didn't look well, but surrounded by his family and the people he loved, he seemed happy to be with them.

Nikolai tried to speak to her of Vermont, but she was vague when she answered now. She had been given important roles in every ballet they were doing that year. Madame Markova knew exactly how to keep her in St. Petersburg. And Danina and Nikolai had finally agreed not to discuss Vermont again until Christmas, at least until the end of the first part of her season. It was an agreement that pained Nikolai to make, but he did so for her sake.

It turned out to be a blessing that he never left, when his youngest son came down with typhoid in September, and nearly died. And it took all of Nikolai's expertise, and that of Dr. Botkin, to save him. Danina was terrified for the boy, and sent Nikolai letters daily, worrying about the child, and aching for Nikolai's terror as a father, knowing how much he loved his children. It would have been disastrous, she told herself, if they'd been in Vermont and the boy had been ill, or worse. Nikolai would never have forgiven himself, or her, for the tragedy, and would always have blamed himself. And it only made her more certain than she had ever been that it would have been wrong for them to run away to America. There were too many people they loved here, and too many obligations that could not be ignored or abandoned.

Despite her illness of the past year, her dancing had improved even beyond where it had been before. Whenever she danced, people talked about her for days, and her name was known now all over Russia. She was in fact the greatest young ballerina of her day. Nikolai was desperately proud of her, and more in love with her than ever. He came to her performances whenever he could, and in November met her father and one of her brothers. There were only two left now, and the other had been recently injured, but was in Moscow, recovering well.

Her father and brother had no idea who Nikolai was to her or how much she loved him, but the three men seemed to enjoy meeting each other. Nikolai wished them luck when they left, and congratulated the colonel on his very talented and remarkable daughter, and the elderly colonel beamed proudly at her. It was easy to see how much he loved her, and he had always known that bringing her to the ballet as a child had been the perfect answer for her. He fully anticipated her being there forever, and it never dawned on him that she was considering leaving it one day.

And when at last Christmas came, Danina couldn't wait to go to Tsarskoe Selo to stay with Nikolai in the little cottage that had begun to seem like their own. It would have been so simple for them if living there could have been a possible solution for them, but it wasn't. They could only be together, on borrowed time, for a few days, or weeks, now and then.

She attended the Czar's Christmas Dance with him. They did not give the grand balls they had before the war, but nonetheless managed to invite over a hundred friends.

Danina shone like a bright star in a gown the Czarina had given her as a gift. It was red velvet trimmed in white ermine, and she looked every bit as regal in it as the Czarina did in hers. Guests all over the room were commenting on how beautiful she was, how elegant, how talented, how gracious, and Nikolai beamed like a handsome prince as he stood beside her, holding her hand.

"I had fun tonight, didn't you?" She smiled as they rode back to the cottage after the party in his sled. They were to have lunch at the palace again the next day. It was a life she loved sharing with him, and she felt almost married to him, standing at his side at the dance. They had been together for nearly two years.

The only thing that had marred the evening at all were the small groups here and there, talking quietly about the echoed rumors of revolution. It seemed absurd, yet the unrest among the populace was exploding regularly now in the cities, and the Czar was still refusing to control it. He said that people had a right to express themselves, and it was good for them to let off steam. But there had been several riots in Moscow recently, and the army was growing increasingly worried. Her father and brother had mentioned it the last time they met.

Danina and Nikolai were talking about it as they walked into the cottage, and this time he admitted to her that he was slowly getting worried about the state of their world.

"I think it's a much greater problem

than most of us realize," he said with a worried frown. "And I think the Czar is being naive in refusing to stop them." Or perhaps he couldn't. He had so many other things to worry about with the war, and the tremendous losses they had sustained in Poland and Galicia, riots in Moscow seemed insignificant compared to the war and what it had already cost them in men.

"The idea of a revolution seems so extreme," Danina said quietly. "I can't even imagine something like that here. What would it mean?"

"Who knows? Maybe not much. Probably nothing. It's a few malcontents making noise. They may burn some houses, steal some horses and jewels, give the rich a spanking, and go back to the way things were. Probably nothing more serious than that. Russia is too big and too powerful to ever change. Although it could make life unpleasant for a while, and dangerous for the Czar and his family. Fortunately they're well protected."

"If anything happens," she admonished him, as he helped her take off her gown in their bedroom, "I want you to be careful."

She realized full well that it could be dangerous for him here.

"There is a simple solution to that problem," he said, broaching the subject of Vermont again. He had promised not to ask her about it again until Christmas, and now the time had come again. And he had given it even more thought since they'd last discussed it in September. It was a recurring theme with Nikolai, and he still hoped to convince her of the wisdom of his plan.

"What solution?" she asked innocently, as she took off her earrings. He had just given them to her, and she loved them. They were pearls with tiny rubies hanging just beneath them, and they looked lovely on her.

"Vermont," he reminded her. "There are no revolutions in America. They don't have a war on their doorstep. We could be happy there, Danina, and you know it." She was running out of excuses not to discuss it with him, and she wanted to be with him, but there never seemed to be a time when she felt ready to leave the ballet, and do something quite so drastic as all that. They were comfortable with the life they shared, and perhaps one day his wife would agree to a divorce.

"Maybe one day," she said wistfully. She wanted to be brave enough to go with him, and yet at the same time she still couldn't imagine abandoning their familiar world. She had an equal amount of elements pulling at her from both directions. Madame Markova and the ballet, and Nikolai and all he promised her. A shared life together in a new land, and the ballet, which was her obligation, her duty, her life.

"You told me you would talk to me about it again at Christmas," he said sadly. He was beginning to fear she would never leave the ballet, and they would never be able to have more than they had now, unless his wife died, or changed her mind, or he inherited a great deal of money, none of which was likely. All she could be here was his mistress, and they could only live together a few weeks a year, unless she left the ballet. But even then, he couldn't have housed her, and they both knew that. Vermont was the only hope they had of being together and starting a new life. But the sacrifices required of each of them still made her shy away from any decision.

"I start rehearsals again after Epiphany . . ." she said vaguely.

"And then you will dance constantly, and it will be summer again . . . and then the fall season, and you will do *Swan Lake* again . . . and then another Christmas. We will grow old together like this," he said, looking at her with loving eyes filled with sorrow and longing. "We will never be together, if we stay here."

"I cannot just walk away, Nikolai," she said gently, just as in love with him as he was with her, possibly even more so, but she understood only too well what he was asking and what it would cost her. "I owe them something."

"You owe yourself more, my love. And me. They won't be there for you when you're old and can't dance anymore. No one will be there for you. Madame Markova will be gone. We must be there for each other."

"I will be," she promised him, and meant it. And with that, he scooped her into his arms, in her elegant silk underwear trimmed in lace, and carried her to the bed where they had first made love, and still took such insatiable pleasure in it. Theirs was a wonderful life, in the brief time they shared, nothing like any other life he had ever known, or any she had dreamed of.

"Perhaps you will tire of me one day," she said sleepily, curled into his arms after they made love, "if we're together all the time."

"Don't worry about that." He smiled, moving so he could kiss her shoulder. Her body was even more beautiful than it ever had been. "I will never tire of you, Danina. Come with me," he whispered again, and she nodded as she drifted off to sleep.

"I will one day," she whispered.

"Don't wait too long, my love," he warned, frightened of a world that was beginning to seem menacing to him. He wanted to leave Russia with her before something happened to all of them. It seemed hard to imagine, but it was possible. There were people in high places now who said so, even if the Czar himself would not admit it. But others that he knew were as

afraid as he was, and he didn't want to ter-
rify Danina. But he wanted to take her
away from it. Before it was too late, before
disaster struck. But he was afraid to say too
much to her. His fears sounded so foolish,
and all Danina knew was the ballet. She
knew nothing of the world beyond it, a
world that was becoming more frightening
every day.

They ate with the family the next day as
planned, and she taught Alexei a magic
trick she'd learned from a young dancer
who had visited them from Paris. And he
was enchanted when she showed it to him.
It was a long happy afternoon, a blissful in-
terlude in their lives. She stayed for more
than two weeks this time, and didn't go
back until the day before rehearsals. She
had kept up her daily exercise, but before
the season there were always long days of
rehearsal that she had to go back for.

"I should go back, to exercise and
warm up," she explained as she packed her
bags on her last day with him. She hated to
leave him, and was pushing her stay with
him in the cottage to its outer limits. But

she had also been dancing so well before their break that she thought she could shave off a few days of practice and rehearsal for the second part of their season. "I hate to leave you," she admitted. They spent the rest of the afternoon in bed after that, making love, and promises, and sharing secrets. She had never been happier with him, and they had never loved each other more than they did at that moment. It was a magical time for them.

And when she left the next day, he promised to come to her next performance.

"We have to rehearse first," she reminded him as she kissed him good-bye at the train.

"I'll come to see you in a few days."

"I'll be waiting for you," she promised. It was one of the happiest times they had ever spent, and she was going to ask Madame Markova if she could have another week away with him in the spring. She was sure that Madame Markova would be furious over it, but if Danina danced well enough in the next three months, she might just agree to it. She was pleased, thus far, that Danina hadn't done anything drastic or foolish, and she was virtually certain now she never would.

The time for that seemed to have gone past them, and Madame Markova was just as sure that eventually they would tire of each other. Letting Danina see him now and then seemed to satisfy them, and in time they would grow bored of an affair that could go nowhere. Madame Markova knew that in Danina's heart, the ballet would win in the end. She was certain of it.

Danina began exercising that afternoon as soon as she got back, and again at four o'clock the next morning, before rehearsal began at seven. She was well warmed up by then, and in good form, and she knew the role well that she was going to rehearse, so much so that she seemed not to pay much attention. In fact, she allowed herself to play a little bit with some of the other dancers, and they clowned around behind the teacher's back, and did some funny kicks and new steps. She did a leap that took their breath away, and then a very pretty pas de deux with one of her partners. And it was late afternoon before they stopped for something to eat. They had been dancing for nearly ten hours by then, which wasn't unusual for them, and Danina was tired, but not excessively. She gave a last leap on her way out, and someone gasped as she slipped and sailed across the floor with one foot at a shocking angle. There was a long silence in the room as everyone waited to see her get up, but she was very white and very still, as she simply lay there and held her ankle in silence. And then everyone ran to her, and the teacher came briskly across the floor to see what had happened. She was hoping to see a bad sprain, or a balle- rina who would be very sore the next morn- ing at rehearsal.

But what she saw instead was Danina's foot almost at an impossible angle to her leg, and Danina clearly in shock and barely conscious.

"Carry her to her bed at once," the woman said sharply. Danina's teeth were clenched, her face deadly white, and there was no doubt in anyone's mind what had happened. She had broken, not sprained, her ankle. A death knell, if it were true, for a prima, or virtually any dancer. There was not a sound, not a word, only the occasional gasp from Danina, as they moved her, and a moment later she lay on her bed, in her leotard and the warm sweater and leg warmers she had been wearing. Without a word, the teacher cut her leotard off, using a small sharp knife she carried for purposes such as that, and the ankle was already swelling to the size of a balloon, the foot still at the same hideous angle, as Danina stared at it in silent horror, the reality too terrible to imagine.

"Get a doctor. At once," a voice said from the doorway. It was Madame Markova. There was a man they used for such things. He was extremely good with feet and legs and bones and he had helped them before, with good results. But what Madame Markova saw as she entered the room nearly broke her heart. In a single instant, with one swift leap, it was over for Danina.

The doctor came within the hour, and confirmed the worst to them. The ankle was badly broken, and she had to be taken to the hospital. They would have to operate in order to set it. There was no argument, nothing anyone could say. A dozen hands touched hers as they carried her away. Everyone cried, but no one harder than Danina. She had seen it happen too often before. She knew exactly what had just occurred. After fifteen years in these sacred halls, for her, at twenty-two, it was over.

They operated on her that night, and the entire leg was set in a huge cast. For anyone else, it would have been considered a success. The leg would be straight again, and if she had a limp from it, it would only be a small one. In her case, that was not good enough. The ankle had been shattered, and even if she walked normally, she would never be able to dance as she had before. It would not carry her weight sufficiently to do what she would have to do. There was simply no way of repairing it to give her the flexibility or the strength she needed. And there were no words to console her. Her career had ended with that one small, foolish leap. Not only her ankle, but her life shattered in a single instant.

She lay in her bed and cried that night, almost as hard as she had when she lost

Nikolai's baby. The life she had lost this time was her own. It was the death of a dream, a tragic finish in counterpoint to a brilliant beginning. And this time Madame Markova sat beside her, holding back her own tears. Danina had made the sacrifices, the vow, the commitment, but the fates had not been kind to her. Her life as a ballerina, the life she had lived and breathed and been willing to die for, for fifteen years, was gone.

She was sent back to the ballet the next day, to lie in the room she shared with the others, and they came to visit her, alone and in pairs, with flowers, with words, with kindness, with sorrow, almost as though to mourn her. She felt as though she had died, and in a way she had. The life she had known, and been an integral part of, had died for her. She already felt as though she didn't belong here. And it was only a matter of time before she had to gather up her things and leave them. She was even too young to teach, and she knew she couldn't anyway. It was not in her. For her, it was simply over. The death of a dream.

It took her two days to write to Nikolai, and when her letter reached him, he came at once, unable to believe what had happened, although everyone explained it to him in detail once he arrived. All the other dancers knew him and liked him. And they told him again and again how she had fallen and how she looked as she lay on the floor.

But seeing her, lying there, with her huge cast, and the look of sorrow in her eyes, said it all to him when he first saw her. But to Nikolai, as ghastly as it was for her, it seemed almost like a ray of hope. It was her only chance for a new life. Without this, she would never have left. But he knew he could say none of that to her. She was in deep mourning over her career.

And this time, when he insisted on taking her away with him, Madame Markova offered no objections. She knew it would be kinder for her not to be at the ballet, for a while at least, listening to the familiar bells and sounds and voices going to class or rehearsals. Danina no longer belonged here. She could return eventually, in some other way, but for now, it was more compassionate not to have her there at all. As quickly as possible for her sake, the past had to be buried. Two thirds of her life, and the only part she had ever cared about until Nikolai, had just ended. Her life as a ballerina was over and gone.

# Chapter 9

*D*anina was immensely relieved to return to their cottage to recuperate, and the Czarina was pleased to see her. Danina's recuperation was slow this time, and painful. And when they finally took off the cast after more than a month, the ankle looked weak and shrunken. She could barely stand on her left leg, and she cried the first time she walked across the room to Nikolai. Her limp was so severe, her entire body seemed distorted. The graceful bird she had once been seemed completely broken.

"It will get better, Danina, I promise," Nikolai tried to reassure her. "You must believe me. You will have to work hard on it." He measured both her legs and found that they were still the same length, the limp was due only to weakness. She would never dance again, but she would walk normally. And no one was more solicitous than the Czarina and her children.

It was several weeks before Danina could walk across the room without a cane, and she was still limping when she received a letter at the end of February that Madame Markova was ill. She had a mild case of pneumonia, but she had had it before, and Danina knew full well how dangerous it could be. In spite of still being unsteady on her legs, she insisted that she had to go to her. She still used the cane to cover distances, and could not walk far, but she felt that she should go back to stay at the ballet, at least until Madame Markova regained her health after the pneumonia. The older woman was frailer than she looked, and Danina feared for her life.

"It's the least I can do," she insisted to Nikolai, but although he sympathized, he still objected. There had been riots in St. Petersburg, and in Moscow, and he was uneasy having her go back alone. And Alexei hadn't been well, so he didn't feel able to go to St. Petersburg with her. "Don't be silly, I'll be fine," she insisted, and after a day of arguing back and forth, he finally agreed to let her go without him. "I'll come back in a week or two," she promised him, "as soon as I see she's better. She would do, and has done, as much for me." He understood all too well the power of the relationship between them, and he knew that Danina would have been agonized over not going to her.

He took her to the train the next day, warned her to be careful and not overtax herself, handed her her cane with a kiss, and put his arms around her. He hated to see her go but understood it, and made her promise to take a taxi directly to the ballet from the station. He was sorry not to go with her. And after all their time together recently, it felt odd to him not to do so. But Danina had promised him she would be fine alone.

But much to her surprise, when she reached St. Petersburg, she saw people milling about in the streets, shouting and demonstrating against the Czar, and there were soldiers everywhere around them. She had heard nothing of it in Tsarskoe Selo, and was amazed to find the atmosphere in the city unusually tense. But she forced it from her mind as she made her way to the ballet. Her thoughts were on Madame Markova, and she hoped her mentor and old friend was not desperately ill. And she was dismayed to find that in fact she had been, and as had happened once before, she had grown very weak and very frail from her illness.

Danina sat beside her every day, fed her soup and gruel, and begged her to eat it. And within a week, she was relieved to see some slight improvement, but the older woman seemed to have aged years in a few brief weeks, and she looked intolerably fragile as Danina looked at her lovingly and held her hand.

Nursing her, the days seemed to fly past her, and Danina fell into bed at night feeling utterly exhausted. And moving around as much as she had, had caused her ankle to swell painfully again. She was sleeping on a cot in Madame Markova's office, her old bed having long since been assigned to another dancer. She was fast asleep on the morning of March eleventh, when crowds gathered in the street not far from the ballet. The shouting and the first gunshots woke her, and she rose quickly and went downstairs to see what had happened. Dancers in the long hallway had already left the classrooms where they'd been warming up, and a few of the bravest ones were peeking from the windows, but they could see nothing but a few soldiers galloping past on horseback. No one had any idea what had happened until later that day when they learned that the Czar had finally ordered the army to quell the revolution, and more than two hundred people had been killed in the city. The law courts, the arsenal, the Ministry of the Interior, and a score of police stations had been burned, and the prisons had been forced open by the people.

The gunshots had stopped by late afternoon, and in spite of the alarming news of the day, that night seemed relatively peaceful. But in the morning, they heard that the soldiers had refused to follow orders and shoot into the crowds. They had retreated, in fact, and returned to their barracks. The Revolution had started in earnest.

A few of the male dancers ventured out into the street later that afternoon, but they returned very quickly, and barricaded the doors of the ballet. They were safe there, but there was shocking news from beyond their little world, and it grew more horrifying day by day. On March fifteenth, they learned that the Czar had abdicated on behalf of himself and the Czarevitch, in favor of his brother, Grand Duke Michael, and was on his way back to Tsarskoe Selo, from the front, by train, to be arrested. It was impossible to understand, much less absorb, what was happening all around them. Like the others, Danina was unable to understand all that they heard. The information was conflicting and confusing.

It was fully a week later, on March twenty-second, when Danina finally got a hastily scribbled note from Nikolai, brought to her in the hands of one of the guards who had been allowed to leave Tsarskoe Selo. "We are under house arrest," it said simply. "I am able to come and go, but cannot leave them. All of the Grand Duchesses have the measles, and the Czarina is desperately worried about them, and Alexei. Stay where you are, stay safe, my darling, I will come to you when I can. And I pray that we will be together very soon again. Know always that I love you, more than life itself. Don't venture out in the midst of this danger. Above all, stay safe until I come. With all my love, N."

She read the letter again and again, and held it in trembling hands. It was beyond belief. The Czar had abdicated, and they were under house arrest. It was impossible to believe it. And she was desperately sorry she had left them. If they were to be in any danger, she would have preferred to be with him. To die with him, if need be.

It was late March when Nikolai finally came to her, looking exhausted and disheveled. He had come on horseback all the way from Tsarskoe Selo, but it had been the only way he could travel. The soldiers guarding the Imperial family had allowed him to leave, and promised he could return. But he had a look of desperation as he sat with her in the corridor outside Madame

Markova's office, and told her in no uncertain terms that, as soon as they could arrange it, they would have to leave Russia.

"Terrible times are coming. We have no idea what will happen here now. I have convinced Marie she must take the boys and go home. They will leave next week. She is still English, and they will allow her safe passage, but they may not be as kind to us, if we stay here. I want to wait until the girls are well over the measles, and make sure that the family is safe. And then we'll arrange to go to America, to my cousin Viktor."

"I can't believe this." Danina was horrified as she listened. It seemed as though in a matter of weeks, their whole world had come to an end. "How are they? Are they very frightened?" She was so worried about them. They had been through so much in the past month, and Nikolai said, with a look of concern, "No, they are all remarkably brave. And once the Czar returned, everyone became very calm. The guards are quite reasonable, but the family cannot leave the grounds now."

"What will they do to them?" Her eyes were full of fear for her friends.

"Nothing, certainly. But it has been a great shock, and a sad end. There is talk of their going to England, to their cousins there, but there is a great deal of negotiation to do before that. They may go to Livadia, while they wait. If so, I will accompany them, and then come back to you. I will arrange passage to America as soon as possible. You must prepare yourself, Danina." This time there was no argument, no discussion, no weighing the decision. Danina knew with utter certainty now that she would go with him. Before he left her that night, he pressed a roll of bills into her hand. He told her to pay for their passage, and arrange it in the next few weeks. He was sure that by then, the Imperial family would be comfortably settled, and he would be able to leave them and go with her.

But she watched him go that night with a feeling of terror. What if something happened to him? As he mounted his horse, he turned and smiled at her, and told her not to worry, and assured her that, staying with

the Imperial family, he would be even safer
than she was. He rode off again at a gallop,
and clutching the money he had left her,
she hurried back into the safety of the
ballet.

It was a long, anxious month waiting to
hear from him again, and trying to glean
what they could from the rumors they all
heard in the streets, from citizens and
soldiers. The Czar's fate still seemed un-
sure, and there was talk of their staying at
Tsarskoe Selo, going to Livadia or going to
England to stay with their royal cousins.
There were constant rumors, and the two
letters she had from Nikolai told her nothing more than she already knew. Even in
Tsarskoe Selo nothing was definite or certain. No one knew where or how it would
all end.

Danina was careful with her funds
while she waited to hear further from Nikolai, and with a terrible pang of guilt she sold
the little nephrite frog Alexei had given her,
knowing that once they were in Vermont,
they would need the money.

She managed to contact her father
through his regiment, and in a brief letter,

told him what she planned to do. But once again the letter she received from him held bitter news. The third of her four brothers had been killed. And he urged her to do as Nikolai suggested. He remembered meeting him, though he still had no idea that he was married, and told her to go to Vermont, and he would contact her there. She and Nikolai could come back to Russia again when the war was over. And in the meantime, he told her to pray for Russia, wished her godspeed, and told her he loved her.

She was in shock as she read his letter, unable to believe that yet another of her brothers had been lost. And suddenly she began to feel that she would never see any of them again. Every day was an agony, worrying about her family, and Nikolai. She bought their tickets on a ship due to sail at the end of May, but it was the first of May before she heard from Nikolai again. And his letter was once more painfully brief, as he hastened to send it as quickly as he could.

"All is well here," he wrote reassuringly, and she prayed that he was telling her the truth. "We continue to wait for news.

Every day they tell us something different, and there is still no definite word from England. It's rather awkward for all of them. But everyone is in good spirits. It looks as though they will be leaving for Livadia in June. I must stay with them until then. I cannot desert them now, as I'm sure you understand. Marie and the boys left last week. I will join you in St. Petersburg, I promise, by the end of June. And until then, my darling, stay safe in our love, and think only of Vermont, and our future there. I will come to see you for a few hours, if I can."

Her hand trembled as she read the letter, and as she thought of him, the tears coursed down her cheeks. For him, for them, for her lost brothers, for all the men who had been lost, and all of their lost dreams. So much had happened, an entire world had ended all around them. It was impossible to think of anything but that.

She exchanged their tickets the next day, for a ship sailing for New York at the end of June. And she explained to Madame Markova what she was doing. Her teacher had regained her strength by then, and like

everyone else now, she was deeply concerned about the future. And she no longer
objected to Danina's plans to leave with
Nikolai. She could not dance with them
anymore, and the danger in St. Petersburg,
and everywhere in Russia, was considerable
these days. Madame Markova was relieved
for her, and she finally admitted that she
believed Nikolai would be good to her,
whether or not they were married, although
she hoped that one day they would be.

But even in the comfort of knowing she
was leaving with him for safety in a month,
Danina was constantly haunted by all that
she was leaving behind. Her family, her
friends, her homeland, and the only world
she knew at the ballet.

Nikolai had already told her that his
cousin had offered him a job in his bank.
They were going to live with him in his
house, for as long as they had to, until they
could afford to live somewhere else. It was
at least comforting to know that. And Nikolai was planning to take the classes he had
to, so that eventually he could practice
medicine in Vermont. It all seemed carefully planned, although Danina knew that it

would take a long time to achieve their goals. But just then, getting out of Russia was the only thought occupying her mind. Vermont itself seemed so distant, it might as well have been on another planet, it was so far removed from their world.

It was a week before they were due to sail, when Nikolai came to see her again, once again with bad news. The Czarina had fallen ill a few days before, she was exhausted, and under a great deal of strain. And although Dr. Botkin was still with them, Nikolai didn't feel able to leave, as planned. Their trip to Livadia had once again been delayed. It was scheduled now for July, as they continued to wait for their English cousins to agree to let them go to England. But thus far, their English cousins had made no commitment at all.

"I just want to get them settled," Nikolai explained, and it sounded reasonable to her. They sat together for an hour, embracing each other, and kissing, and just feeling the comfort of being close. And while Danina sat with him, Madame Markova made him something to eat, which he gratefully devoured. It had been a long, dusty ride from Tsarskoe Selo.

"I understand, my darling, it's all right," Danina said calmly, holding fast to his hand. She only wished she could go back to Tsarskoe Selo with him, to see them all again. She wrote the Grand Duchesses and Alexei a quick letter, sending them her love, and promising that they would meet again, and Nikolai folded it carefully and put it in his pocket, to take it back with him.

He had explained all the circumstances to her, and what the house arrest entailed. They were allowed to walk in the gardens, or anywhere on the grounds. And he told her that people stood at the gates and stared at them, talking to them sometimes, telling them they loved them, or criticizing them for what they had or hadn't done. Just listening to him talk about it was painful to Danina, and she wished more than ever that she could be in Tsarskoe Selo with them, to lend them her support as well, and just be there for them.

She hated to see Nikolai leave again that night, but knew he had to go back. And this time, she exchanged their tickets for a boat leaving on the first of August. Nikolai had promised to be back in St. Petersburg by then. It was incredible to her to realize that they had already waited three months to leave, since the Revolution began. It seemed an eternity to her now as she continued to wait for him.

By then, some of the dancers had gone home to other countries, other towns, but most of them had stayed. All their performances had been canceled months before, but once she was well again, Madame Markova insisted that classes continue as usual. She invited Danina to watch with her, and little by little, Danina's limp had begun to fade, but there was no question of her ever dancing again. But for the moment, she no longer cared. All she could think of, as the days crawled by, was Nikolai, and their friends. And it was the end of July when Nikolai returned. And this time, he said, the plans for the Imperial family were certain. The trip to Livadia had been vetoed by the provisional government as too dangerous for them to undertake, as they would have to pass through what were deemed

hostile towns, and they were leaving for Tobolsk in Siberia on August fourteenth. But
as he said it, Nikolai looked cautiously at
her. There was more he had to say, and he
wasn't sure how Danina would react to the
decision he had made.

"I'm going with them," he said, so
softly that at first she felt sure she hadn't
understood him.

"To Siberia?" She looked shocked.
What was he saying? What did it mean?

"I have gotten permission to go with
them on the train, and return here immediately afterward. Danina, I cannot leave
them now. I must see this through to the
end, and see them to safety. Until they hear
from their cousins in England, they will stay
in exile in Tobolsk. Livadia would have been
far more pleasant for them, but the government wants them as remote as possible, for
their own safety, they claim. The family is
terribly distressed over it, and it only seems
fair to go with them. You must understand.
They've been like family to me."

"I do understand," she said, her eyes
filling with tears. "I am just so sorry for
them. Are the guards decent to them?"

"Very much so. Many of the servants have gone, but other than that, inside the palace at Tsarskoe Selo, very little has changed." But they both knew Siberia would be different, and like Nikolai, Danina was worried about Alexei. "That's why I want to go," he said quietly, and she nodded again. "Botkin is going too, and he will stay with them. That was his choice, and in a way, it frees me to leave and come back here." But as she nodded again, gratefully, he still had more to say. "Danina," he began, and she sensed something ominous in his tone, before he even said the words to her. She could almost guess what he was going to say. "I don't want you to exchange our passage again. I want you to go this time. It is too dangerous for you here. Something can happen, particularly right here in town. And I can't come to you, or protect you, when I'm that far away." On his way to Siberia, there was no way he could help her. Even now, getting from Tsarskoe Selo into St. Petersburg had become an endless ordeal. "I want you to leave for America on August first, as we planned, and I will go to Siberia with them in a few weeks, and sail on my own as soon as I can get back to St. Petersburg. I will feel much better knowing you are there, and Viktor will take care of you. I don't want any arguments, I want you to do as I say," he said, looking almost stern, anticipating the resistance she would offer him, but she surprised him this time, and with tears streaming down her cheeks, nodded at him.

"I understand. It is dangerous here. I will go . . . and you will come as soon as you can." She knew there was no point arguing with him. She knew he was right this time, although it pained her terribly to leave without him. But if he was going to Siberia with the Czar, perhaps it was best that she leave before that. "When do you think you will come?"

"No later than September, I'm sure of it this time. And I will be much happier knowing that you are safe and far from here." He put his arms around her then and held her as she cried, longing for the time when they would be together again. He already knew that Marie and the boys were safe, and happy to be in England. Now he wanted to know that Danina was safe too. He knew that his cousin would take good care of her. Viktor had already promised to do whatever he could for them. And Nikolai trusted him completely. He knew that Danina would be in good hands with him. It would relieve Nikolai's mind as he accompanied the Imperial family to Tobolsk, and then returned to St. Petersburg. And then he would sail to America to be with her, and their new life would begin.

He had told Marie his plans before she left, and she had been surprisingly understanding about it, and promised he could visit the boys anytime. But Nikolai knew, as did she, that it might be years before he could come back to Europe. But the farce that was their marriage had gone on for long enough, and in his heart, he was more married to Danina than to Marie. The legalities, and the papers, no longer meant anything to him. Marie had wished him well when she left, and the boys had cried, as had he. Marie had been dry-eyed, relieved to leave Russia at last, and in her heart she had long since relinquished him. He felt free to move on now, as soon as he had fulfilled his obligations to the Imperial family.

"I will come back here in a day or two," he said to Danina, before he left her, "and we can stay in a hotel until you leave." He wanted to be with her again, to lie with her, to hold her in his arms, to see her safely on the ship. It would only be a month or so before they were together again after that. But before she sailed, he needed to be with her. It had been five months since she had left Tsarskoe Selo and returned to St. Petersburg when Madame Markova fell ill, and it felt like a lifetime to both of them. Their entire world had changed totally in those five months, and would again when they met in Vermont. Nothing would ever be the same for them again, but perhaps better now, he prayed. He would have preferred to leave with her, but his conscience would never have allowed it. He had to see the Imperial family to safety first. He owed them at least that much after all their kindness to him, and the many years he had served them.

He left, as planned, that night, and returned to St. Petersburg three days before

Danina was to sail. She was watching a class with Madame Markova when he arrived, and one of the students came in on silent feet to find her. Danina looked up instinctively and saw Nikolai watching her from the doorway. She knew then that the good-byes she dreaded were about to begin, and that it was time for her to leave. And she felt Madame Markova stiffen as she sat beside her. Danina looked at her for a long moment, and then walked slowly to him, with no trace of her limp. Her bags were packed, in the room where she slept, and she was ready. And as she put away the last of her things, while he waited in the hall, Madame Markova came to join her, and stood looking down at her valises. Everything Danina owned had fitted easily into two old battered cases, and as she stood to look at her mentor, neither of them spoke for a long moment. Danina did not trust herself to speak, and the woman who had been like a mother to her for fifteen years looked stricken.

"I thought this day would never come," the older woman said in a voice that quavered. "And I never thought I would let you go, if it ever happened. . . . Now I am happy for you. I want you to be well and happy, Danina. You must leave here."

"I will miss you so," Danina said, taking two long strides to her, and putting her arms around her. "I will come back to see you." But in her heart, Madame Markova knew she wouldn't. She could not believe, as she looked at the child she loved, a woman now, that she would ever come back here. And she knew to the very depths of her soul that this was their final moment.

"You must never forget all you have learned here, what it meant to you, who you were when you were here . . . and who you always will be. In your heart, Danina, take it all with you. You cannot leave this behind you. It is part of you now."

"I don't want to leave you," Danina said, sounding anguished.

"You must. He will come to you when he can, in America, and you will have a good life with him. I believe that. I wish it for you."

"I wish I could take you with me," Danina whispered, clinging to her, wanting to stay forever.

"You will take me with you . . . and a part of you will always be here with me. Here." She pointed to her heart with a graceful finger. "It is time now, Danina," she said, pulling away from her, and picking up one of the valises, as Danina took the other, and followed her slowly from the room into the hallway where Nikolai waited. He could see instantly how difficult the moment was for them, and went to relieve them both of the valises.

"Are you ready?" he asked Danina gently, as she nodded, and walked to the front door, as Madame Markova followed slowly, watching her, savoring each final second.

And just as they reached it, the front door opened, and a child walked through it. She was eight or nine, and she was carrying a suitcase, as her mother stood proudly beside her. She was a pretty child with straight blond braids, and she looked expectantly at Danina.

"Are you a dancer?" she asked boldly.

"I was. I'm not anymore." It cost Danina a great deal to say it, as Nikolai and Madame Markova watched her.

"I'm going to be a ballerina, and I'm going to live here forever," the child said with a smile.

Danina nodded, remembering the day she had come. But she had been so much more frightened than this child, so much less sure, and also considerably younger. But she had had no mother to accompany her.

"I think you'll be very happy here," Danina said, smiling at her through her tears, as Madame Markova watched her. "You have to work very, very hard. All the time. Every day. You have to love it more than anything else in the whole world, and be willing to give up all the things you love to do, and want, and have and think . . . this has to be your whole life now." How did you explain that to a nine-year-old? How did you make them want it more than anything else in life? How did you teach them to sacrifice and give until they nearly died? Or did you even teach it? Did they have to be born to it? Danina didn't have the answer. She simply touched the child's head as she walked past, and looked up at Madame Markova with tears in her eyes.

She knew even less how to say good-bye, after the years of sacrifice, the years of giving and loving. How did you give it all back when it was over? But for her, it was the end of the story. The dance was over. For this child, it was just beginning.

"Take good care of her," Madame Markova said softly to Nikolai, as the child and her mother walked past them. And then with a last touch of Danina's hand, Madame Markova turned and walked solemnly away, so they wouldn't see her cry. Danina stood and watched her for a long moment, and then walked slowly out the door for the last time, one foot after the other, until she stood outside, like everyone else in the world. She was no longer part of the ballet, she no longer belonged there, and never would again. This was the moment she had dreaded all her life, and it had come now. She was no longer part of their world, she was leaving them forever. There was no changing that, no turning back, as the door closed silently behind her.

# Chapter 10

*T*hey spent their last day in St. Petersburg walking the streets, going to places they had both been fond of. It was a litany of memory and torment, and suddenly Danina could no longer remember why she was going. They both loved it here so much, why would they want to leave? But they could not delude themselves anymore. It was dangerous here. Their time in Russia was over. There was no way they could ever have had a life here. Even less so now, with the Revolution in full progress. But without it, Marie would have stayed, and held on to him. Danina would have had nowhere to go without the ballet. They had to go thousands of miles away, to a new world, to have a life together. And they both knew it was worth it. It was just excruciatingly painful leaving. But in another day, she'd be on the ship, in a month he would come too, and they could begin their life together. In some ways, it seemed like a great adventure. But she was still desperately sad to leave him in Russia.

For the moment, they were staying at a hotel, under his name, and on their way back, they bought a newspaper, and read with dismay of the war news. And all of it was distressing. It was impossible to ignore.

They had dinner in their room that night, clinging to each other for the last moments they could share, wanting to be alone for their final hours. They had so much to say to each other, so much to dream of, and promise. The days and nights they shared went all too quickly. They barely slept those last three days, not wanting to miss an instant with each other. Her bags were all packed, her few treasures and souvenirs ready to go with her. And he was sending two bags of his with her too, as though to prove to her that he was coming later. She was even bringing the gowns the Czarina had given her, although she knew they were part of the past now, as it all was.

Danina wondered at times how they would ever explain to their children, if they had any, what their lives had been. It would all seem like fairy tales to them, as it did to her now. Perhaps all one could do, in the end, was forget it, put the souvenirs away, the programs from the ballet, the photographs, the gowns, the toe shoes, and dust them off now and then to look at them. Or perhaps even that would be too painful. She knew that when they left St. Petersburg she would have to close the door on the past forever.

They went to bed early the last night, and lay in each other's arms all night, barely sleeping. But the sun rose all too quickly, and they left their bed for the last time with a look of sorrow. Danina was already anticipating the loneliness of his absence.

The porter carried her bags downstairs for her, and the two trunks she was taking for him as well, and she felt like a child leaving home forever, as the door closed softly behind her.

"I promise you, Danina, I'll come soon, no matter what the situation here. Nothing will stop me." He read her mind and reassured her in the car on the way to the ship. It made her feel sick with worry to leave him, especially knowing he'd be traveling to Siberia with the Czar and Czarina and their children, and then back to St. Petersburg again.

He helped her board the ship, and settled her into the cabin. She was to share it with another woman, but she hadn't arrived yet, and Danina chose the bunk she wanted. But she barely left Nikolai's side and was suddenly dreading the crossing, and said so. Without him, she would be desperately lonely, and constantly afraid for him.

"I'll miss you too," he said, smiling lovingly at her. "Every moment. Take good care of yourself, my darling. I'll be there in no time." She walked back up to the deck with him when the boat horn sounded to warn visitors to go ashore, and he stood holding her for a long moment. It no longer mattered to either of them who saw them. In their own eyes, they were man and wife. "I love you. Remember that. I'll come as soon as I can. Give my love to our cousin. He's a bit dull, but very kind. You'll like him."

"I'm going to miss you dreadfully," Danina said, with tears in her eyes, unable to hold them back.

"I know," he said softly, "so will I." He kissed her long and hard then as the boat horn sounded for the last time, and they began to remove the gangplanks.

"Let me stay with you," she said breathlessly in his arms, trying suddenly to convince him. "I don't want to leave you. Perhaps they'd let me come to Siberia with you." She would have done anything to stay with him.

"They'd never let you, Danina, you know that." He didn't want to tell her it was dangerous, but that was not a secret to them either. He wanted her safe in Vermont now, no matter how much he wanted to be with her.

"Just remember how much I love you," he reminded her. "Remember that until I join you. I love you more than anything in life, Danina Petroskova. . . ." It was the last time he would ever call her that.

They had already agreed that in Vermont she would use his name, Obrajensky, so no one would ever know they weren't married.

"I love you so much, Nikolai." And as she said it, instinctively she touched her locket. It was there, safely at her neck, beneath her sweater.

"I'll see you soon," he promised for a last time, kissed her quickly, and then hurried down the last gangplank, as she went to the rail and watched him leap to the dock and stand there, watching her.

"I love you!" she shouted. "Be careful!!" She waved at him and he waved back, mouthing "I love you" at her. And moments later, the big ship began to move slowly from the dock as she felt her heart pound, and wondered why she had been stupid enough to let him convince her to leave without him. Everything about it felt wrong to her, but she knew she had to be brave now, for his sake. They had been through so much together, she could do just a little more, let him finish his work here, give his last to the Imperial family, and then join her in Vermont, to begin their life together as man and wife.

She waved to him until she could barely see him anymore. He was still standing there, waving at her, tall and proud and strong, the man who had won her heart two years before, and whom she knew she would love forever.

"I love you, Nikolai," she whispered into the wind, and then stood there for a long time, with tears running down her cheeks, thinking of him and holding her locket. She wasn't even sure why she was crying. He was right. They had so much to look forward to, so much to be thankful for, so much waiting for them in Vermont. It was all beginning. She had no reason to cry, except that in a place in her heart she was desperately afraid that she had just seen him for the last time. But there was no reason to think that. It was foolish, she told herself, as she looked up at the sky and saw the last gulls flying past. She could not lose him now. It could not happen. And with a sigh, and a last glance at her homeland, thinking of him, she walked slowly down to her cabin. She could not lose Nikolai, she told herself. No matter what happened to them, she would always love him, there was no way they could lose each other now.

# *Epilogue*

*T*he answers, as they always are, were right in my backyard. I had the letters translated, and they were all love letters from Nikolai Obrajensky to my grandmother. They covered a span of time, and told a story that touched my heart, almost as much as it had touched hers for a lifetime. The letters explained it all very clearly.

The rest I learned from two of her friends, neighbors, when I went back to Vermont the following summer to see the house, and spend a week there with my children and my husband.

I found the Czarina's gowns in a trunk in the attic, and never knew they had been there. They were still in the same trunk she had brought them in, they were all faded, and the ermine was yellow, and more than sixty years past their time, they looked like costumes. I was surprised I had never found them in my childhood forays, but the trunk was old and battered, and hidden in a corner of the attic. His trunks were there as well still, two of them, neatly labeled DR. NIKOLAI OBRAJENSKY. She had never had the heart to unpack them once she arrived in Vermont.

The programs from the ballet had new meaning for me now, the photographs of her with the other dancers. And the toe shoes seemed somehow sacred. I had never realized how important they were to her. I knew she had danced, but had somehow never understood what she had given of herself to do that. I tried to explain it to my children, and their eyes grew wide when I told them the story. And when I showed Katie the toe shoes, and told her they'd been Granny Dan's, she leaned over and kissed them. It would have made my grandmother smile to see that.

And just as she had feared when she set sail in September 1917, she never saw

Nikolai again. He went to Tobolsk, in Siberia, with the Imperial family, as he'd promised to, and got trapped there. After that, he was no longer allowed to leave, and remained under house arrest with them. His devotion to them had ultimately cost him his freedom, and in July 1918, he was executed with them. A brief letter from a name I didn't recognize informed her of it four weeks later. I can only imagine what reading that letter must have done to her. And I sobbed all these years later, when I read the translation. She must have felt as though she would die without him.

But before he had died, his last letter had warned her that there was talk of an execution. Cruel as it may have seemed at the time, he had tried to prepare her. He sounded surprisingly cheerful actually, and strong, and had told her that she must go on, that she must find happiness in her new life, and remember him, and their love, with joy and not sorrow. He told her he had been married to her in his heart since they'd met, and she had given him the happiest years of his life, and his only regret was not leaving with her. She must have known that day, that she would never see him again. And yet, destiny could not be altered. Neither his, nor hers. She was destined for another life, with all of us, in a place so far from the life she had shared with him. And he was not destined to be with her.

Her father and remaining brother were killed at the end of the war. And Madame Markova died of pneumonia two years after my grandmother last saw her.

She lost them all, one by one, irrevocably, lost everything, a life, a country, a career, a handful of precious people . . . the man she loved, her family, and the dancing she had loved so much before that.

Yet there had never been anything tragic about her, nothing sad, or sorrowing, or mournful. She must have missed them terribly, especially Nikolai. Her heart must have ached from time to time, and yet she never told me. She was simply Granny Dan, with her funny hats, and roller skates, her sparkling eyes, and delicious cookies. How could we have been so foolish? How could we have thought that that was all of her, when there was so much more? How could

I have believed that the little woman in the frayed black dresses was the same person she once had been? Why do we think that old people have always been old? Why could I not imagine her in the red velvet gown trimmed with ermine, or dancing *Swan Lake* for the Czar in her toe shoes? And why did she never tell me? She had kept all her secrets to herself.

She lived with Nikolai's cousin for eleven months, waiting for Nikolai, and another month until she knew he had been executed. As Nikolai had promised, his cousin was kind to her. A quiet man, with his own memories, his own regrets, his own losses. She must have been like a ray of sunshine to him. He was twenty-five years older than she. Forty-seven when she arrived at twenty-two. She must have seemed like a child to him. And he must have always known how much Nikolai meant to her. Five months after Nikolai died, sixteen months after she had come to Vermont, she married Nikolai's cousin, my grandfather, Viktor Obrajensky. And to this day, I don't really know if she ever loved him. I assume she did. They must have been friends. He was always kind to her, although he said very little, and she spoke of him with tenderness and admiration. But I couldn't help wondering now if she had loved my grandfather as she had loved his cousin. I somehow doubt it, though in her own way, I think she loved him. Nikolai had been the passion in her life, the dreams of her youth, so soon ended.

So much I never knew . . . so many dreams I never could have imagined. She was indeed a mystery. I have the pieces now . . . the trunk . . . the shoes . . . the locket . . . and the letters. . . . but she kept the rest with her, the memories, the victories, the people she loved so much. My only regret is how little I knew about her when I was with her, how ignorant of her past.

Granny Dan, the woman she was to me, will live on in my heart forever. The woman she was before that belonged to other people. They took her with them, and she kept them close to her, in her heart, in her spirit, in letters and a locket. She must have loved him still to take the letters to the nursing home with her, and the locket with his picture. She must have read the letters even then, or perhaps after so many years of reading them, she knew them by heart.

And now, when I close my eyes, she is not old . . . her dresses are not black or frayed . . . she is no longer baking cookies . . . she is smiling at me, as young and beautiful as she once was . . . and she is dancing in her toe shoes, as Nikolai Obrajensky smiles, and watches. And I believe that somewhere now, they are together at last.

*D*ANIELLE STEEL has been hailed as one of the world's most popular authors, with over 390 million copies of her novels sold. Her many international bestsellers include *Bittersweet, Mirror Image, The Klone and I, The Long Road Home, The Ghost, Special Delivery, The Ranch, Silent Honor, Five Days in Paris,* and other highly acclaimed novels. She is also the author of *His Bright Light*, the story of her son Nick Traina's life and death.